Catherine Cookson wte daughter of a povert he believed to be her ol ce but eventually moved d married Tom Cookso At the age of forty she he working-class people with whom she had grown up, using the place of her birth as the background to many of her novels.

Although originally acclaimed as a regional writer – her novel *The Round Tower* won the Winifred Holtby award for the best regional novel of 1968 – her readership soon began to spread throughout the world. Her novels have been translated into more than a dozen languages and more than 50,000,000 copies of her books have been sold in Corgi alone. Many of her novels have been made into successful television dramas, and more are planned.

Catherine Cookson's many bestselling novels established her as one of the most popular of contemporary women novelists. After receiving an OBE in 1985, Catherine Cookson was created a Dame of the British Empire in 1993. She was appointed an Honorary Fellow of St Hilda's College, Oxford in 1997. For many years she lived near Newcastle-upon-Tyne. She died shortly before her ninety-second birthday in June 1998 having completed 104 works, nine of which are being published posthumously.

'Catherine Cookson's novels are about hardship, the intractability of life and individuals, the struggle first to survive and next to make sense of one's survival. Humour, toughness, resolution and generosity are Cookson virtues, in a world which she often depicts as cold and violent. Her novels are weighted and driven by her own early experiences of illegitimacy and poverty. This is what gives them power. In the specialised world of women's popular fiction, Cookson has created her own territory'
Helen Dunmore, *The Times*

BOOKS BY CATHERINE COOKSON

NOVELS

Kate Hannigan

The Fifteen Streets

Colour Blind

Maggie Rowan

Rooney

The Menagerie

Slinky Jane

Fanny McBride

Fenwick Houses

Heritage of Folly

The Garment

The Fen Tiger

The Blind Miller

House of Men

Hannah Massey

The Long Corridor

The Unbaited Trap

Katie Mulholland

The Round Tower

The Nice Bloke

The Glass Virgin

The Invitation

The Dwelling Place

Feathers in the Fire

Pure as the Lily

The Mallen Streak

The Mallen Girl

The Mallen Litter

The Invisible Cord

The Gambling Man

The Tide of Life

The Slow Awakening

The Iron Façade

The Girl

The Cinder Path

Miss Martha Mary Crawford

The Man Who Cried

Tilly Trotter

Tilly Trotter Wed

Tilly Trotter Widowed

The Whip

Hamilton

The Black Velvet Gown

Goodbye Hamilton

A Dinner of Herbs

Harold

The Moth

Bill Bailey

The Parson's Daughter

Bill Bailey's Lot

The Cultured Handmaiden

Bill Bailey's Daughter

The Harrogate Secret

The Black Candle

The Wingless Bird

The Gillyvors

My Beloved Son

The Rag Nymph

The House of Women

The Maltese Angel

The Year of the Virgins

The Golden Straw

Justice is a Woman
The Tinker's Girl
A Ruthless Need
The Obsession
The Upstart
The Branded Man
The Bonny Dawn
The Bondage of Love
The Desert Crop

The Lady on My Left
The Solace of Sin
Riley
The Blind Years
The Thursday Friend
A House Divided
Kate Hannigan's Girl
Rosie of the River
The Silent Lady

THE MARY ANN STORIES

A Grand Man
The Lord and Mary Ann
The Devil and Mary Ann
Love and Mary Ann

Life and Mary Ann
Marriage and Mary Ann
Mary Ann's Angels
Mary Ann and Bill

FOR CHILDREN

Matty Doolin
Joe and the Gladiator
The Nipper
Rory's Fortune
Our John Willie

Mrs Flannagan's Trumpet
Go Tell It To Mrs Golightly
Lanky Jones
Nancy Nutall and the Mongrel
Bill and the Mary Ann
    Shaughnessy

AUTOBIOGRAPHY

Our Kate
Catherine Cookson
    Country

Let Me Make Myself Plain
Plainer Still

Rosie of the River

A NOVEL

CATHERINE COOKSON

CORGI BOOKS

ROSIE OF THE RIVER
A CORGI BOOK : 978 0 552 14712 5

Originally published in Great Britain by Bantam Press
a division of Transworld Publishers

PRINTING HISTORY
Bantam Press edition published 2000
Corgi edition published 2001

13

Set in 11/13pt Sabon by
Phoenix Typesetting, Ilkley, West Yorkshire.

Corgi Books are published by Transworld Publishers,
61-63 Uxbridge Road, London W5 5SA,
a division of The Random House Group Ltd

www.randomhouse.co.uk

Addresses for companies within
The Random House Group Limited can be found at:
www.randomhouse.co.uk/offices.htm

The Random House Group Limited Reg. No. 954009

A CIP catalogue record for this book
is available from the British Library

Printed in Great Britain by
Clays Ltd, St Ives plc

Rosie of the River

PART ONE

Early Days

I

It was on the twenty-eighth of August 1950 at eleven thirty p.m. that Fred Carpenter said to his wife Sally, 'Darling, it's a complete rest you need. You can't go on burning the candle at both ends.'

'It's too late for a holiday,' she said: 'we haven't booked one.'

'Well' – he stretched his neck out of his collar – 'there's always the Broads.'

Sally looked sharply at him. 'Don't be silly, dear. You've got to book up months ahead there.'

'There are such things as cancellations; we could always enquire. There's no harm in that.'

'But there's only another fortnight before the school term begins.'

'Well, we could have a week . . . Just imagine: weather like this, hot sunshine, no wind, and practically empty rivers. It's nearing the end of the season; there can't be many people there now.'

'But you know nothing about boats, Fred.'

His neck moved further out of his collar. 'I know as much as the next. There are two old Broads books in the attic. We sent away for them last year. Don't you remember? And I'm not a dim-wit altogether.'

'No, dear; you're not; and if I remember *we* didn't send for the books, *you* did.'

His head subsided. 'Yes. Yes, I suppose I did . . . Why didn't we go then?'

'Because I put *my* foot down for a change: I can't swim and I don't like boats.'

'But you've learnt to swim since.'

'I can do four breast strokes before I make for the bottom.'

'Don't be silly. You're getting along fine. And look' – his head began to ascend again – 'I'm going to put *my* foot down now. If I don't, I can see I'll soon be living on my own.'

'You wouldn't be living alone long; some other idiot would soon feel the urge for self-sacrifice.'

'There' – he did a bit of strutting up and down the kitchen rug – 'you see what I mean? You're all on edge. It's this shop that's wearing you down, working there morning, noon and night; you've only given yourself a break now because business is quiet.'

'Morning, noon and . . .' Sally was lost for words. 'I still manage to do everything in the house, just as it always has been done. It's my job that keeps me sane.'

'Well, I don't care what you say, you're going to have a break, now that you've got these two weeks free. We're going.'

As there didn't seem to be much more to be said, they went to bed.

At nine, the next morning, a Saturday, Sally stood at the kitchen door listening to him phoning Blake's boatyard, and her heart sang when his doleful voice came to her, saying, 'You've got nothing, nothing at all?'

There followed a buzz, buzz, buzz, and then his voice again, a little on the defensive now, 'Yes, I know it's late, but we didn't know we could make it . . . illness and one thing and another, you know.'

His wife raised her eyebrows to the ceiling at this whopper.

When he came into the kitchen he sat down without a word.

'What did they say?' she asked.

'You heard. They're full up to the end of the season.'

His disappointment was so intense that she almost began to feel sorry for him.

'Well, if you really want that kind of holiday we'll book early next year,' she said, knowing full well that from this day forth she would plan to spend whatever holiday they were to have on very dry land. But still feeling sorry, yet a bit of a hypocrite, she added, 'You should have left them with our phone number in case anything should crop up.'

'I did.'

'Oh.'

Sally made her way to the scullery and the dishes. Then by way of an enticement, she said, 'If you get on with the painting and finished the house this holiday it would leave you clear next year and we could . . .'

The chair scraped hard on the lino.

'I suppose it would.'

His exit was as curt as had been his reply. The door slammed, the ladder outside banged against the wall, scraped along one of the upper windows, making a screeching noise, and she just stopped herself from rushing out and crying, 'For heaven's sake! Be careful!'

At half past ten the phone rang, and she went to it quite gaily. It might be one of a number of friends; or it might be one of the dozens of local schoolboys who had forgotten he was on holiday and wanted a word with his favourite teacher 'Mr Chips'. How she loathed that nickname for Fred.

It was neither of these, it was the man from Blake's office in London. A cancellation had just come in for a three-berth cruiser. Weren't they lucky?

Weakly she said there were only two of them . . . Whereupon the man said, 'Well, madam, it'll go like hot cakes.'

She checked the appropriate retort.

The phone was in the hall, and her husband had a phobia about it. Nothing would induce him to answer it, even if he was passing when it rang. She could be in the bath, and frequently had been, when he had yelled, 'Phone!' And she'd had to tear downstairs wet and shivering in her dressing-gown and answer a boyish squeak enquiring for 'Mr Chips'.

Now, to get from the top of the ladder to her side he must have leaped down the fourteen rungs, and he arrived just at the moment when a great temptation was not only assailing her but had all but conquered her. The phone was snatched from her hand, and in his politest tones, he said, 'Carpenter here. You've got one?'

The voice from the other end replied, 'It's for three . . . twenty-nine pounds . . . *Dogfish Three*, that's its name. Lovely little craft, at Oulton Broad.'

'Good! Yes, by all means five pounds deposit. Yes . . . Yes, take-over four o'clock, Saturday. Fine. Thank you very much . . . Yes, we are very lucky . . . Goodbye. Goodbye.'

Sally found herself swung round the hall, danced round the kitchen to 'A Life on the Ocean Wave', and plumped into a chair. Gone was the curtness, gone was the wife-driven, house-painting husband. Here was the merry, jolly boy, and the merry, jolly boy took her face between his hands until her lips did prunes. Then he stuck his two index fingers into the sides of her mouth and pulled her face up into a smile.

'Come on. Come on. It's going to do you the world of good. Make a new woman of you.'

'What about the concrete for the drive?' was the reply. 'We were to give up a holiday now to get that done.'

'Oh, honey, the drive'll be here when you're not; you're goin' to have a holiday.'

'We'll not do it under forty pounds, and we can't afford it. And the concrete an' all . . .'

'Damn the concrete! And we'll do it on thirty-five . . . you'll see.'

'Bill!' It was a cry from Sally's heart, and she looked towards the corner of the kitchen where, in an outsize in dog baskets, was lying an outsize in bull terriers.

'Bill? . . . Bill? My God, yes! Oh, Lord.'

Bill was the love of their lives, all his sixty pounds; but he was also the worry of their lives. He was possessed by only two passions: one kind for people, another for dogs. The first was an endearing passion, the second was a tooth-and-gore emotion. Bill's temper had been broken completely when, as a pup, his best friend, a big labrador, turned on him over the small matter of a bone, and left his face in ribbons. From that day every dog became suspect, and a great deal of the Carpenters' life was spent keeping Bill in the garden and other dogs out.

At this point Bill rose, waddled over to them with his hippo roll, stretched out his back legs, and laughed.

'We could try the Poynters; we could say he's quietened down.'

'You know he hasn't,' said Sally.

'We could ask Mrs Chapman.'

'No. Much as Mrs Chapman likes Bill she wouldn't take him. They've only got a tiny garden.'

'The Brunnel Kennels; I'll try them; they've got a good name.'

The phone phobia was apparently conquered for the moment.

Away he went, and in less than no time Fred came back. 'Why,' he asked his wife, 'are kennel folk always snooty? Lord, you'd think they boarded earls and film stars instead of dogs. Their bookings for this month were closed in June! Huh!'

Hope again rising quickly, Sally said, 'Well, we just can't go, that's all. You'll have to write and tell them. Anyway, we haven't sent the deposit; we'll lose nothing.'

'What!' Every inch of Fred's five feet five slowly became elongated, and his eyes, as he looked at her, turned from grey to a deep steely blue. This was a phenomenon that had happened in the past. And when it happened she always gave up, for the Gladiator was once more in possession.

She had a theory about her husband. She was positive that in one of his previous incarnations he had been nothing less than a gladiator, for how else could he achieve the things he did with his five feet five inches and nine stone? He tackled jobs as sidelines that other men took life-times to learn, and he always wanted to do them unaided.

She had suggested before that on each of his achievements he place a plaque inscribed 'Alone I Did It'. But of all the schemes he had thought out and of all the things he had done, none had, up to date, been so mad or so foolhardy as the idea that she now knew he was about to put into terrifying words.

And there they were, thrust on to the air, from their very birth portending disaster, bringing countless innocent, pleasure-bent people trouble and worry, letting loose tempers, unleashing elemental desires that would otherwise have lain quietly buried in the sub-conscious.

'Bill,' he said, 'comes with *us*.'

Bill was one person's full-time work when he

was hemmed in by a fence; loose on a boat, God help them!

Sally believed firmly that dogs had a soul, and that a third of it was of human quality, and this was further proved to her by Bill's immediate response. He looked up at the two beings who were his gods and whose company he would have torn through the entire regiment of Crufts to reach, and at one and the same time his head, ears and tail slowly dropped; and, still with his eyes upon them, his bandy legs sagged until he finally lay down with a plop. Bill knew that his transportation to a boat could mean nothing but disaster for them all.

'That's settled, then,' said the Gladiator.

Bill lowered his eyes from Sally's. Yes, he and the Gladiator's wife both knew it was settled.

For sanity's sake, over the next three days, Sally could not bear to think of the times that Fred confronted her with the list of things to take on board. Apparently everything she tried to pack for herself would not be needed; all she would need would be shorts, two jumpers, a nightdress and a face flannel.

His own requirements were a pair of old shorts for oiling in, a decent pair of whites for steering in, a pair of something decent in the shorts line to go ashore in. He applied the same system to his shirts, vests and pants. But when his wife asked about shoes, he said, 'Shoes? The only shoes I'll take will be what I go in. My camping plimsolls will be all that's necessary. You don't use shoes on a boat, dear . . . rubber! Rubber soles every time.'

'No slippers at all? You're always complaining about your Achilles heel.'

'Tendon.'

'Well, whatever it is, don't you need your slippers?'

'No.'

'Very well . . . Now, about food. Will I pack up what's necessary?'

His hand went to his head as he said, with studied calmness, 'It was agreed we are travelling light.'

'But you said we'd take most of our food . . .'

'It'll be better to get the odds and ends we'll need at the boat station.'

'But I've got piles of home-made jams and tinned stuff here already. It would save money.'

'What money? About thirty bob. Is it worth it?'

'Very well. Have it your own way.'

They travelled what Fred called 'light', with two large cases, a despatch case, a leather carrier-bag, a handbag, and Bill. In the taxi taking them to the station they discovered they had forgotten the tin-opener, and the Broads book had said bring a tin-opener.

Both felt guilty on that journey about Bill. The poor dear was wearing a muzzle for the first time: it was Fred's idea to save Sally worry, and it was to be worn in stations only and when crossing London. Bill loved people, but from Hastings to London he found no-one to love but his owners, for although the train was crowded everyone gave them a wide berth, and they had the carriage to themselves. However, apart from a few wisecracks such as that of the taxi driver, who said, 'Sure you don't want a cattle truck, missus?' they arrived at Liverpool Street without mishap, and actually boarded their train to Norfolk the minute it came in, only to find that every seat in their particular section was reserved. It would have been all the same had they all been empty, for the guard turned out to be a man who wouldn't believe that the muzzle was absolutely unnecessary, so Bill was relegated to the guard's van; and since his owners flatly refused to leave him, they also were relegated to the guard's van. As it turned out, this was a blessing in disguise, for every other compartment of the train seemed to house a dog, although it was only when they were nearing Oulton and could still hear the yapping that Sally said to her husband, 'Where are all those dogs going?'

'What a silly question to ask,' he said. 'How should I know?'

Three hours of squatting in the guard's van had tested his charm.

'They are not making for the boats on Oulton, are they?'

'Don't be stupid,' he replied. 'All those dogs!'

'Well, we brought him, poor soul.' Sally pointed to the poor soul, for no-one could look such a poor soul as Bill when he felt he was not getting a square deal; and to her mind, to muzzle any kind of a dog was anything but a square deal. If a dog had to be muzzled it was done because it would bite people, not dogs. She felt he was being convicted for the wrong offence.

The station at Oulton was small, and when they arrived there wasn't a taxi in sight, only a boy with a home-made, boy-powered truck. And he had already been commandeered by a large man with a large family and six cases.

When the Carpenters enquired how far the boat station was, they were told, 'Along there and just over the bridge.'

Fred, off his hunkers and on his feet again, was once more the jolly sailor boy. He led the way, carrying the cases, and Sally followed with the bags, the despatch case and Bill, whose every extremity was once more feeling the pull of gravity.

'Don't worry, darling,' she said to him, 'we're nearly there, and we'll soon have that nasty muzzle off you.'

'Excited?' Her husband threw the word over his shoulder.

'Not very.'

'Oh, you will be as soon as you see the boats bobbing . . . "When the red, red robin comes bob, bob, bobbing along." '

'Fred! Not here . . . please!'

His head went back and he let out a bellow of a laugh.

Fred could not sing; it was the one problem on which he had failed to make an impression; he was tone deaf. Moreover, although he had an excellent head for mathematics, he could not remember more than one line of any song, hymn or ballad without being prompted. 'It was a night, Oh what a night it was!' was more often than not followed by 'Sons of William Parker', which happened to be the school song of the educational establishment in which he taught. This could be followed by anything from 'Abide With Me' to 'We Shall Gather At The River'. It was the last that now floated on to the Oulton air. And it was too much for Sally.

He stopped, put down the cases and beamed his approval of her laughter.

'That's more like it! Oh, we are going to have a week; I can feel it in my bones.' His hand emphasised this statement by administering a hearty whack across her backside.

Her laughter disappeared. 'You're in the street, remember. And stop acting like the Englishman abroad.'

'I'll act how I damn well like. Come on.'

Not more than a few steps along the street they were brought to a stop; Fred had an idea. 'Look,' he said, 'give me your bags and things, and I'll go on to the boatyard, settle up with the chap there and get aboard while you get some odds and ends of eats.'

'What about Bill?'

'Well, you don't expect me to lug him along too, now, do you?'

'No. But I would rather you were in the vicinity if something happens.'

'There you go again . . . looking for trouble. What can happen? He's muzzled. All you've got to do is hold on to him.'

Holding on to him, Sally went into a general store. It was a very nice one, and as she looked round she saw that she needed a lot of things. One of the assistants, an elderly lady, came up to her. 'Can I help you, madam?' she asked. Then glancing sideways at Bill, she added, 'Does he bite?'

'No, no; he's as gentle as a baby.'

The eyes of all the customers were turned in her direction, and not one of them looked as if they thought there was any truth in her statement.

'What can I get you, madam?' asked the assistant.

She got tea, sugar, butter, bacon, potatoes, milk, bread, Nescafé, grapefruit, peas, oranges, marmalade, apples, cheese, salt, pepper, custard powder, jam biscuits, cake and sausages.

Bill was lying at his mistress's feet like a lamb, confirming her description of him and giving the lie to the looks that were being bestowed on him. The stores were mounting up on the counter in front of her, and she began to feel a spark of excitement. Then the assistant asked, 'Shall I send them to the boat for you, madam?'

'Oh, yes, please.'

The woman took a piece of paper. 'What is the name?'

'Carpenter.'

'Of the boat, madam.'

Sally looked at the woman. 'The boat?' Good Lord! She didn't know it. At least, she explained in confusion, she had heard it, but forgotten it. She was about to explain how all this boat business had come upon her like a flash of lightning when a tiny snigger from behind made her turn. Two ladies, evidently pukkah Broads *mesdames*, were amused, and a male customer eyed her with what she thought was a funny look, not the kind that she usually received as the wife of a grammar-school master. At this point, Bill arose, wagging his entire body; and there, in the doorway, was Fred.

Smiling her relief, she cried, 'Darling, what is the name of our boat?'

'*Dogfish Three.*'

He came across the shop laughing, and she could see he was in high good humour: 'Trust you to forget where you live,' he was saying; and as he reached her side he playfully patted her behind.

The two ladies eyed each other, and the exchange spoke volumes. The man continued to stare. But now he was looking from Sally to Fred. Perhaps he was wondering why she should have picked a small man. Sometimes she wondered herself, for this Jekyll and Hyde character made life with him an uncertain business: when she thought she was dealing with the cheerful boy, she was suddenly confronted by the sombre schoolmaster. At this moment she would have preferred the schoolmaster; but the jolly boy was still to the fore.

'What a nice lot of eats! Sausages. Good! Did you get anything for lunch tomorrow?'

'No.'

'Would you like a chicken, madam?'

The assistant darted away and returned with a cooked chicken the size of a well-fed pigeon.

'How much?' Sally asked.

'Fourteen shillings. There's a lot of cutting on it . . . it's compressed.'

Sally would have agreed with that, but the compression certainly didn't refer to the price. She was about to decline with thanks when Fred put in, 'That'd be nice. Get some green stuff; we'll have chicken salad.'

She got some green stuff, and they paid the bill
. . . three pounds one and sevenpence ha'penny.
By this time the shop assistant was all smiles and
referring openly to Fred. This often happened;
at times Sally had wondered why he did not go
in for snake charming.

He further pleased the assistant by dispensing
with the services of the boy who was to carry the
stuff to the boat and who was undoubtedly very
busy. The assistant loaded Fred with a cardboard box piled high and Sally with a
carrier-bag.

All this while they were being watched by the
tall man.

As Fred was at his most flippant, Sally had not
thought he had noticed the man, until, outside,
he remarked, teasingly, 'That fellow never took
his eyes off you. What have you been up to? I
can't leave you alone for a minute.'

'That bill was three pounds one and seven,'
she said crossly. 'We were going to live on thirty
shillings for the week, d'you remember? As for
the man, he imagines, I think, that I am either
your permanent dim-witted mistress or a pick-
up, certainly not your wife, which idea you did
your best to confirm with your handplay.'

'So you imagine he imagines that? What a mind you have, woman. But don't you like being taken for somebody's mistress? Not many women with a white streak in their hair could be, you know. And stop being so prim; you sound like a sentence out of a book. Anyway, what d'you expect in that get-up?' He eyed her hat.

It was a small affair, made entirely of flowers, and Sally knew that, without any false modesty, it became her. Her suit was a plain one, a very plain one: she had paid quite a bit for its plainness.

'What's wrong with my get-up?' she asked.

'Nothing. But I should imagine you're the only woman in Oulton with a hat on. Or a rig-out like that. They're all in slacks or shorts.'

'So I've noticed,' his wife retorted. 'And they look ridiculous, like female stowaways in a Robert Louis Stevenson novel.'

He laughed and pointed: 'Look! There's the Broad. Wait till you see the boat; she's a little beauty. Isn't this a nice little town, everything spick and span? . . . Here, stop that!' The last was a command to Bill, who had let out a baritone growl and was standing like a ramrod, tail and nose in line and every brindle hair protesting its individuality. A few yards away, and coming out of what looked a delightful little park and walking with soft, wary, padded steps, was another bull terrier, but a pure white one, and ugly.

'Ssh! Get away! Go on with you.' Fred moved towards the enemy, who appeared totally unaware of his existence and came steadily on, and Bill, deciding to meet him half-way, took a spring, which lifted Sally clean off the pavement and onto the asphalt fronting the park.

Holding on for dear life, she yelled, 'Throw something at it! Hit it with a stick or something.'

Handicapped with the box, Fred kicked out in a deterring movement. But still the horrible beast came on. And then, with a terrific snarl, he sprang . . . Both dogs sprang.

Whether it was by accident or design that Fred dropped the box of groceries no-one could tell, but it saved the day. It must have hit both of the dogs' heads at one and the same time, for with two different kinds of yelps they sprang apart.

It was unfortunate that Sally wasn't quick enough in taking the same line, for meeting the retreating force of Bill, she sat down suddenly in the gutter; and whether the groceries rained down on her before, simultaneously, or after, she did not know. But bags, tins and packets struck her at all angles. And there they were, spread around her, as were also a number of kindly residents.

But she was still in charge of Bill; and that was everything.

Once more on her feet and being dusted down, she watched her husband restore the groceries to the box. She noticed one person who did not offer his assistance. He was the man from the shop. He must have witnessed the humiliating scene from across the road. And now there was an entirely different look in his eye.

Whatever she may privately have thought of Fred she would not stand for anyone pitying her for being saddled with him; and there was undoubtedly pity in the man's eye. There were scores of people who imagined that her husband was wonderful, such as the worried mothers of little boys at school, who sought his advice, and stopped her in the street to tell her what a wonderful husband she had. And, whatever her private opinion, no tall, lean, hungry-looking individual was going to pity her. She returned the man's stare with hauteur – he had the grace to move on. After thanking their helpers and trying to vindicate Bill's character, the Carpenters too moved on – there was only one thing Sally wanted now and that was to get them all safely onto that boat.

Fifteen minutes later they were aboard. Bill was tied to the iron leg of the adjustable table, and the cabin was full of Sally and the baggage . . . As for Fred, he was everywhere.

She sat down on a nice Dunlopillo seat and surveyed what was to be their home for the next seven days. To be strictly truthful, she was agreeably surprised. The main cabin was eight feet four inches long; the table dropped to form the centrepiece of a double bunk; beyond was a galley and small dining area in which the seats let down to make a third bunk. Further on was a lavatory and wash-basin, then a door leading to the open stern area.

From where she was sitting two steps led up to what she supposed was called the wheel-house. It was covered with a canvas awning or hood.

She bent down and patted Bill. 'Nothing is so bad that it couldn't be worse,' she said. 'If all goes well, we may even enjoy ourselves.'

Bill could not be persuaded to agree. He could

not believe that she had forgiven him in so short a time. His feelings were delicate, and once hurt, took time to recover.

She began to unpack, interrupted by glances through the window. High above them was the neat green and white Commodore public house, while all around lay boats, big ones, little ones, fat ones, and slim ones, berthed so close as to be touching.

On each side of the Carpenters were the companion boats to theirs, *Dogfish One* and *Dogfish Two*. This, Sally found, was very interesting, and she was about to open the cabin door to draw Fred's attention, when a sailor barged down the two steps almost knocking her over, turned his stern to her, lifted up the step he had just come down, grabbed a handle, worked it up and down a number of times, cried, 'OK,' banged the step back again, then jumped back up into the well and disappeared onto the roof of the cabin. She could follow his travels by the sound of his feet just above her head.

Leaning against the table, she looked down at Bill, who was now on his feet, with his tail hovering at an undecided angle. Like his mistress, he also thought he knew that sailor . . . But Fred was slimmish, he didn't possess an

34

outsize in a seaman's jersey, and he certainly did not possess a sailor's hat, a real sailor's hat, either new or old, and the one Sally had just seen was old, very old, and dirty, and spoke of countless voyages.

She waited, not moving. The door burst open again, and now the sailor grinned at her.

'What on earth?'

'Now, now, now!'

'You look like . . .'

'Now don't say it.'

'You look like a bus conductor.'

'What! Have a heart. A bus conductor?'

'Where on earth did you get that hat?'

'Cap, darling.'

'Where did you get it?'

'In Hastings.'

'Hastings?'

'Yes, where we live, remember?'

'But why?'

'Well, I saw it in a second-hand shop, and I thought, That's just the job.'

'But it's filthy; you don't know who's worn it. And you're the one who won't even dry your hands on anyone else's towel.'

'I sterilised it.'

'You sterilised it?'

'Well sort of. I wiped the inside of the lining with disinfectant.'

'You're mad. How is it that I haven't seen it before?'

He grinned. 'I stuffed it in my raincoat pocket.'

'Where did you get the jersey?'

'I had to buy it.' His grin broadened.

'But where?'

'Just now. At the Yacht and Caravan Supply Company along the street . . . it's a nice shop.'

'But you haven't had the time.'

'Well, I got it. There's a spring left in me yet.'

'You are mad.'

'You said that before . . . and come on and get out of that suit and hat. Come on' – he shook her arm – 'come up on deck. The man's coming back to show me the ropes. Ropes . . . that reminds me. How long is it since you did any jumping? You'll have to jump around for the next week.'

'Jump? Where?'

'Off the boat, of course, with the rond anchor, when we moor. You'll either have to take her in or jump off, take your pick. So come on now, the quicker you learn the better.'

She wanted to protest that this holiday was

to be a rest, yet the thought was burrowing rapidly into her mind that for the next seven days she'd be alone on a boat on a wide river with Fred, and from past experience she felt it would be only common sense to be ready for all emergencies.

So, still in her flowery hat and her very plain suit, she went on deck. And there, almost it would seem in the same room, so close was he, was the lean, hungry-looking man, not now dressed as she had seen him, but in a spick and span shirt and shorts; and standing beside him was his wife . . . Sally had not misjudged him, the woman looked like his wife. And leaning over the side of their boat doing something with ropes was a lanky youth of about sixteen, definitely their offspring. They were all tall and lean and hungry-looking, and she thought that here was another instance of the phenomenon of married couples taking on each other's looks after having lived together for some time. The evidence of this family resemblance made her more determined still to keep her own individuality and her extra inch from making her appearance like Fred's.

Being of a forgiving nature, and preferring to get along with people, even to the extent of overcoming her prejudices, she was about to bestow on the lanky family a smile, when the lady, after one long, significant stare, turned on her heel and went below. She was followed immediately by her husband, leaving only their son to stare. And stare he did. There seemed to be nothing he hadn't inherited from his father, and Sally had an uneasy feeling that his staring wasn't without point. She and Fred, there was no doubt in her mind, had been under discussion, and she thought, tartly perhaps, that the tall man had used her as a parable to press home the facts of life.

She wrenched herself from the youth's fixed stare and turned her attention to the wheel.

An engineer from the boatyard had arrived on board and was instructing Fred on the equipment.

'This,' he was saying, 'is simple. Can you drive a car, sir?'

There was a slight pause. Then, 'No,' said Fred truthfully.

'Well, that doesn't matter. This top lever here is the throttle, and that knob below is the ignition switch. And that one there is the self-starter. And this lever is the choke. And that little one above is your cockpit light. This here is your gear lever. It's detachable, look, and lifts out easily. Your petrol switch is down there, under the locker. There's your Calor-gas tank under the back seat. Your clean-water tank's in the bows; and that's the lot, sir. If you don't mind I'll leave you a minute, but I'll be back to take you out.'

He jumped onto the quay; and, dazed, Sally went below.

Pretending not to be confused, Fred followed.

'Did you get all that?' he asked.

'No. Did you?'

'Of course.' He laughed. 'And don't look so green. Put your faith in the skipper.'

She sat down heavily. 'I wondered, when I was doing it,' she said, 'what prompted me to make a will and send it to my sister.'

'You didn't! You're not serious?'

'I did.'

'You haven't much faith in me, have you?'

Gone was the jolly boy, and back was the serious, harassed, middle-of-term schoolmaster. And looking at his face she felt mean. Why had she tried to spoil his fun?

'Oh, darling.' She was on her feet. 'It's just that you get so excited about things – no-one would believe it – and then things happen.'

Somewhere between the top of the roll-neck jersey and the lower peak of the cap, she kissed him, aware all the while that the schoolmaster's face did not suit the naval rig-out.

'Don't you think I'm entitled to let up sometime? I'd go bats if I didn't. Forty weeks of youth a year make an old man of even the youngest of us.'

'Oh, I know, darling. Come on, I'm sorry. Enjoy yourself.'

The wife – or mistress – was thrown aside: she was the mother now, coaxing, pleading. 'I'll tell you something,' she said. 'You don't look a bit like a bus conductor. It suits you.'

The faintest of smiles appeared.

'Honest?'

'Honest.'

Suddenly they laughed and threw their arms about each other, and kissed again; and even as their lips met, they turned, forced round by a feeling of intrusion. And there, wearing varied expressions, was the entire Lean family looking at them through the two sets of windows.

'That,' Sally said, jumping back, 'has torn it. They think we aren't married. I can tell by their faces. Why can't we behave like ordinary people?'

Fred bellowed with laughter, his equable temper entirely restored. 'Let's keep them guessing. You know, deep in my subconscious I suspect I've always wanted to be the kind of fellow who runs a mistress as a sideline.'

'Fred!'

'All right, Sal.' He shook his finger at her. 'Don't forget you're the one who enjoys plays and novels about the wiseness of being frank ... The Wiseness of Being Frank.' He laughed. 'That's a good one . . . nearly up to *The Importance of Being Earnest*.'

Running mistresses as sidelines, and everything else, was at this instant swept away from Sally's mind as she yelled, 'Bill!'

The cry had been torn from her when, like a streak of lightning, Bill's heavy body flashed out of the cabin. At just a little below lightning speed, Fred followed.

It was the tackle which more than anything else had earned him his place in his college's rugger team at Oxford, and he had almost lost the technique through disuse until they had acquired Bill. But during the past eighteen months he had put it into action so often that now his practices amounted to a couple a week.

Bill did not like being caught by the tail. Sally

thought much of his sensitivity must be stored in that section of his body, for he always responded very quickly when it was grabbed as Fred grabbed it now. His reaction was to sit down and try to return the compliment. But a yell of 'No!' from his master had up to now turned the grab into a nibble, which had been fortunate.

She was unable to get out of the cabin because her husband's feet, heels up, were blocking the doorway. But leaning over him, her hands on the floor, she could see all she wanted to see.

The Lean family had a dog. It was a black nondescript mongrel, and it was standing, forepaws on the rim of their boat, looking calmly down on Bill in all his humiliation, and it wore exactly the same expression on its face as the one which was prevalent on those of its owners – curiosity coupled with disapproval.

'Come along, darling,' Sally coaxed anxiously. 'That's it, be a good dog.' The tone she used to Bill caused the boy's mouth to open, his mother's to close tighter, and his father's to pull in at the corner.

But Bill's reaction was more disturbing. He barked.

Now Bill rarely barked during the day. Even

when he went into a fight it was accompanied only with a low growl. They had always tried to stop him barking, for his bark was one of the most head-splitting, piercing sounds known to man. And now, even though he was being held firmly by the collar and both of them were yelling, 'No!' he gave it full rein, and such was its force it caused the Lean faces to screw up in protest. Not so that of their dog. For it answered Bill with a shrill piping yap. This seemed to act on Bill as a spur, for his bark became louder and more piercing, if that was possible. Then horror on top of horror: gradually from every part of the Broad, so it seemed, a dog joined in the chorus.

'Out of the way!' yelled Fred, as, tugging with all his might, he pulled Bill down into the cabin again. But this did not quieten Bill's voice, and Sally implored him from her knees, where her husband had thrust her, 'Bill. Bill, darling. Oh, Bill, give over.'

'I'll Bill him . . . Shut up, you damned animal!' Apparently deafened by his own voice, Bill did not hear that of his master, and was only silenced when Fred, pulling the strap off a case, brought it smartly down across his nose. Sally, too, winced at the sting, but it did the trick.

There was silence, at least in their boat. But now they could hear more clearly the noise coming from outside and from all around. It was fantastic. Every note and shade of dog bark was in full blare.

Fred, darting from one window to the other, cried, 'My God! Look at them! It's like Crufts afloat.'

Sally looked. There must have been about fifty boats all told on the Broad, and on the decks of four out of five of them was a barking dog. Some were racing around cabin tops with their owners scrambling after them; some were being pushed into cabins; some were being hit on noses as Bill had been; one she saw swimming around its boat. The peaceful, sunlit water was now a troubled dog-ridden sea.

There was a knock on the cabin door, and the engineer, smiling broadly, for which the Carpenters blessed him, said, 'You ready for off, sir?'

'Yes, yes, the sooner the better. This damned beast started something.'

'Oh, that's nothing . . . very funny, in fact. I'll say, though, he's got some bark, never heard a better. Well, now, sir, you know where the bilge pump is.' He pointed to the steps. 'And that's where you turn your petrol on. D'you remember? And now for your oil – most important this.'

He lifted up the top of a box that looked like a seat and exposed the engine.

'To the left, sir, right down this side is your oil. Pull this out, wipe it, stick it back again and it will show you your oil level.' He held up a slender steel stick and, thrusting his arm down among the machinery, he pushed, then pulled, and held it up covered for about two inches from its end with oil.

'Keep it like that, sir, and it'll be all right.'

'I will.'

'And now we're off,' said the engineer.

'And not before time.' The voice, unmistakably from Manchester and female, came from the cabin of the next boat. 'Bringing a great murderous animal like that on a boat! If ever there was a pair of questionable customers . . . and her decked out as if for the *Queen Elizabeth*.'

'Ssh!'

It was a male 'Ssh!'

Sally reared. 'How – how dare she?' That anyone should question their respectability was bad enough, but that it should be done in a

Manchester accent, a common Manchester accent, was unforgivable. Fred a maths master, a beloved maths master at a grammar school, a kindly, boyish, inoffensive dear, and she, the owner of a ladies' dress shop, and what was more than that, a good housewife, cook and gardener . . . Questionable customers, indeed!

'Laugh at it, honey. We know how funny it is.'

'Funny! *Funny!*' Sally's voice was a squeak.

The engine gave a phut-phut-phutting sound.

Concerned only with the boat, the engineer moved the lever forward, stroked the wheel, and they began to glide slowly out past the Mancunian contingent.

Fred was standing by the engineer's side, and just as their stern left the bows of *Dogfish One* he quoted in a quiet but clear voice to no-one in particular, '*Odi profanum vulgus et arceo.*'

Fred was proud of his knowledge of the classics and more so his knowledge of Latin. As it wasn't his subject he didn't need to know it, for who wants to improve on Latin from their schooldays? Sally got tired of Latin tags, because she didn't understand them, but from the length of this one and from certain of the sounds that had become familiar she knew it was the one about abhorring the unhallowed mob and holding it aloof. And this was one of the rare occasions on which she was glad her husband knew so much.

Her chin went up. She smiled a superior smile, thinking, that puts them in their place, even if they don't know it, when, like a blow in the neck, came the words, still in broad Manchester, 'Horace, Book Three, Ode One.'

She remained stiff and straight. That horrid, spotty boy! Just likely scraped through to a grammar school! And of course he would have to know that very quotation. Book Three, Ode One! Horrible individual!

They circled the Broad, then came back towards the quay again. But the engineer left them before they reached it, jumping onto another craft on which were three scantily dressed girls. One in particular, Sally noticed, had lovely long brown legs, and blond hair falling straight on to her shoulders. She lay looking down on *Dogfish Three* from her vantage-point on the cabin top, then suddenly, to Sally's amazement, she gripped her knees in her hands, pulled them up to her chin, rocked herself, and laughed.

Fred looked towards her, and to his wife's

further amazement and indignation, his laugh joined hers.

'It's your hat, dear. You've still got it on.'

'My hat?' She touched it. 'What is there to laugh at in that? If I want to keep it on I'll keep it on, all night if I like.'

She was angry. Fred, a very dry-land sailor, could dress up ridiculously, and no-one thought him funny, whereas she, wearing an ordinary hat, was laughed at. She stood her ground, and refused to scuttle below and strip off her clothes to conform with the semi-nudity around her.

She stood staring over their cabin top, until the laughter was no longer to be heard. As she stared she became aware of the ripples parting from their bows, and her thoughts were dragged from herself to take in the fact that Fred was alone at the wheel. The boat was under his control, and they were moving smoothly over the water.

Slowly the yachts and cabin cruisers slid away from their sides, together with the gaily flower-decked quayside, and the sun did not seem to be only touching the ripples on the surface, but to have buried its gold deep in the water. They were floating over a sheet of molten metal.

Sally's temper could not withstand it: 'It's beautiful,' she exclaimed softly.

'You've seen nothing yet . . . Now what is he up to?'

The latter part of the remark was meant not for Bill, as one would have expected, but for a cruiser ahead of them, which was weaving first to the right and then to the left.

'What's he playing at?'

'He looks as if he might be trying to avoid those things bobbing about in the water. They might be danger signals.'

'They're not, they're buoys for mooring to.'

'Oh.' Already Fred knew.

They passed the weaving boat, and she saw at once the cause for its unsteady course. The wheel was changing hands a little too often: in fact, a whole family of six was crowded round it, father acting as instructor.

'Fool!' growled Fred.

She glanced at him. He was no longer the jolly boy, nor yet the serious schoolmaster. Another man had been born: the captain on the bridge. Meekly, she went below.

Bill was lying beneath the table, with his eyes popping and his ears up. He rushed at her but was pulled up by his lead. She could see that the throbbing of the engine, which sounded much louder in the cabin, was not to his liking. He nuzzled her hand, butted her with his head, and made another attempt at galloping.

'Look,' she said; 'I'll close the door and let you loose if you promise to behave. And you can look out of the window.'

He did just that. Jumping onto one of the seats, he stood looking down into the fast-moving water as if mesmerised.

Sally finished the ship-shaping and changed into slacks and sweater, and when a hail came from the wheel, she was presentable for the deck. She looked at Bill, who was still water-gazing. He could not be kept in the cabin all the time, that was certain, the poor thing would go mad. So, gripping him firmly by the collar, she opened the door and they both squeezed through and into the well together.

'You know what you're doing, I hope,' said Fred, still in his captain's voice. 'What if he goes over the side?'

'He won't. Will you, dear? Now sit. That's a good boy. Come and sit on this nice leather seat and look at the water.'

Almost like a lamb, he did as he was bidden, and not only did he sit on the seat, but he lay down and, putting his head on his paws, fixed his fascinated stare upon his master.

Sally's spirits rose. He was going to behave. He might even get to like the boat. She dared to leave him and stand beside Fred. Neither of them spoke.

A cruiser passed, going at quite a speed. In it seemed to be three young fellows, all laughing their heads off. When their wash rocked *Dogfish Three* from side to side she caught hold of Bill, and Fred yelled, 'Damn young fools! Five m.p.h. the limit is.'

Thankfully tempers were cooled when another cruiser passed them coming downriver. The man at the wheel and the woman at his side raised a hand in salute, and Fred responded.

'They're nice,' said Sally, 'aren't they? Friendly.'

'It's the camaraderie of the river.'

'It's nice,' she said again.

At this point they rocked violently, and she clutched at the door frame for support.

'Damn fool!' muttered Fred again. 'Five miles per hour, you're supposed to go here. He must be doing ten.'

The camaraderie seemed suddenly to have got caught in the wash.

When they were steady once more, Fred said, 'Get the map, will you?'

Before she obeyed, Sally looked fondly at Bill and remarked, 'Just look at him, isn't he lovely and quiet?'

Fred did not take his eyes from the river ahead to look at Bill, but he said, 'Of course he is. I knew he'd be all right, once aboard. It's you who make him like he is with all your fuss.'

Quivering under the injustice of that remark, his wife flounced below and flounced back, plonked the map on the cabin top and stood in a deep huff. Why was she always blamed for everything? It was unfair, to say the least.

With one hand Fred was tracing his finger along the blue river on the map. He was quite oblivious of her hurt feelings. 'What we've got to look for,' he said, 'are good moorings. We've passed Waveney Hill. There, that on the right. All this is marshland, here.'

Sally looked reluctantly about her: it was indeed marshland. The reeds were higher than the boat, and once again she was brought back to a good temper by the river and its offspring, for the waving reeds were really beautiful. The moss, green at their base, marked the rise and fall of the tide. Immediately above this mark they changed to a biscuit brown, then to a blue green, and lastly, forming an enormous length of rippling mauve velvet, were their heads. They went on and on, a waving barrier to the water. She sighed, and Fred said, 'I told you it would be grand.'

It was, at that moment; but then, they hadn't yet been introduced to Breydon Water and the nightmare of it.

The beginning was when he suddenly said, 'We must find a place to berth and study the map for the tide to get us over Breydon Water.'

'Breydon Water? What's that?'

'Just what it says – a stretch of water.'

'And the tide goes up and down on it?'

'Yes, dear.' He was speaking now as if to a child. 'That's what tides do, they go up and then they come down.'

There was a long pause before she said, 'You'd better be careful, Mr Carpenter.'

He laughed and replied, 'Well, you ask the silliest questions . . . Look! Along there! That looks like a place where we might get in.'

She looked, and replied quickly, 'There are two palings sticking up, as far as I can see.'

'Yes; but beyond them there is a gap and a green bank.'

Slowly and steadily he made for the gap.

When they were within three yards of it he said nonchalantly, 'It's a bit muddy. You take the wheel and ease her slowly to port.'

'Would you mind giving your directions in plain English – left or right?'

'All right,' he said, 'I will, except whilst we are in dock.'

'No!' Sally's voice was loud. 'That's the very place I need you to use plain English, even if it shows you up as a dry-land sailor.'

He swung about, then said, 'Here! Take the damn wheel and keep her to the left.'

Sally took the wheel nervously and watched him grab up the rond anchor and the rope, before jumping onto the narrow gunwale. As he gave a mighty leap, she let out a high squeal, for she was certain he would miss the bank. Fortunately, he only half did so. His upper body caught it, but his legs were dangling in a foot of water.

She had to admire him, for he did not turn towards her but grabbed up the rond anchor from where it had landed.

After stamping it well in, he turned and did look at the boat. At the same time it struck them both: how was he to get back? The depth of water would not allow the boat to be pulled any nearer the bank.

His eye went to the top of the cabin and he cried, 'Turn off the engine!' Then, pointing, he said, 'Pull down that wooden gangway affair from up there.'

The gangway? It must be that plank with pieces of wood nailed across it like a ladder.

'How d'you expect me to get over the awning and onto the roof of the cabin?'

It was in almost a yell that he replied, 'By going through to the stern where there isn't an awning, woman.'

He knew that the word 'woman' always got his wife's back up. She stalked through the cabin to the stern. There, she had to stand on the seat and heave herself onto the cabin top.

Unfortunately, there she stuck, staring down at the long thick plank with strips of wood nailed regularly along its length to be used as rungs.

'How on earth am I going to get this off the roof?'

'By sliding one end over the rail until it drops on to that strip of deck. Then get yourself down and ease it along.'

How she managed it she never knew, but

there it was, end up on the deck, Sally clinging with one hand to the cabin rail and using the other and her knee to ease it along the narrow ledge towards the cockpit.

She had just reached the opening when there was another yell. 'Keep the top end with you. It has two hooks on it which will hold it to the rim of the boat.'

The only way she could accomplish this task was first to straddle the plank and let herself down into the cockpit, and from there manoeuvre the damned thing down.

Looking back again, she had to wonder how on earth she had the nerve to accomplish this – she was petrified by the whole business.

When the end of the plank hit the bank the Captain came up it at a run and, grinning widely, patted her on the shoulder, exclaiming, 'Good work, First Mate! You're a bright lad . . . when you get out of your skirts.'

What Sally meant to say to him was never actually uttered, but her look must have expressed her feelings. However, these were swiftly swept away by the sound that came from Bill, who spoke plainly for himself: Bill was not an animal who would obey the command 'Sit!' One had to press forcibly on his lower back in order to get him to place his nether end on the ground. Perhaps his tail hurt him; but there he was, his rump planted firmly on the deck and, speaking in his own language, he was telling them he was desperate to relieve himself.

'Oh, God!' groaned the Captain. 'He wants to go out.' With an impatient movement, he grabbed the lead, fixed it to Bill's collar, thrust him on to the seat near the plank; then placing his front paws on it, he demanded, 'Up!'

It was as if Bill had suddenly gone deaf, for his rump again was fixed to the seat and his eyes were looking straight into Fred's. 'You're not getting me down that plank, laddie,' he was saying quite clearly.

'Up!' This order was given with a push.

'He's not going to walk down.' Sally's voice sounded quite calm.

'Well, woman,' cried the Captain, 'what do you expect me to do?'

'Carry him.'

'What? Down that plank?'

'Yes; unless you mean to throw him overboard. That's the only other solution.'

'Don't be funny, woman, you know the weight of him.'

'You call me woman just once more, Admiral,

and you'll find yourself over the side.'

They glared at each other. Then with a swift movement, he hoisted Bill into his arms. The poor fellow put his back legs as far round the Captain's waist as possible, and his forelegs around his throat, so tightly that Sally heard a gasp from the Captain, who was now standing on the seat, one hand gripping the iron stay supporting the end of the awning, the other thrust out, aiming for balance as he stepped onto the plank; then he endeavoured to look down the plank, and what he saw did not encourage him to take it slowly, but to get it over at a run. He took three large leaps and landed on the bank on his hands and knees, by which time his burden had jumped aside and was now standing shaking himself.

Sally watched her husband get slowly to his feet, grab the lead and prepare to tug his offended dog along the bank, when Bill himself, tugging sideways, made for the stump of a willow tree, which he proceeded to honour copiously.

This was not Bill's usual procedure: normally, he would have tested a number of trees before deigning to lift a leg. On this occasion, however, he also proceeded to manure its roots. Poor Bill;

by now it was hours since his last time on dry land.

After attempting to dig a hole, he gave up the impossible task, and returned quite quickly to the foot of the plank, and again sat down. The Captain exclaimed loudly, 'Oh, no, fellow! Oh, no! You're going up that plank under your own steam.'

Bill's attitude said plainly, 'The only way I'm going up there is as I came down.'

There was about to be a long discussion, between master and stubborn bull terrier, so Sally suggested, 'Look! I'll lie as far as I can over the side and hold my arms towards him. Lift him on to the bottom rung and give him a push.'

Fred stared at her for a moment; but then, following her instructions in part, he lifted Bill's forelegs onto the end of the plank, and with a force she had not seen him use before, he brought the flat of his hand down on Bill's rump, which caused him to bring his forepaws a further two rungs up the plank; then looking at his mistress's arms outstretched down each side of the ladder, he not only leaped for them but for Sally as a whole, and brought them both with a crack against the cabin side, down which they slowly subsided onto the deck.

'Blasted dog!'

There was a dull pause in her head; then she heard the Captain say, 'Are you hurt, darling?' There was real concern in his voice, and it struck her this was an opportunity she was rarely given, so she managed a gasp and a little moan and found herself being led into the cabin and placed gently on the seat with a cushion at her back, his voice saying, 'Sit still, my love; I'll get you a drop of brandy.'

'Sit still,' he had said, and 'my love'. Sally had no intention of going anywhere, but certainly what she was going to do was to make the most of this very comforting situation . . . She drank the brandy, and when asked, 'Do you feel any better now, dear?' she merely nodded.

This was followed by 'Is your back hurting?' to which she merely gave a slight shake of her head.

When this was followed by her feet being gently lifted onto the seat and a cushion at her head, and Fred's fingers stroking her face while he muttered, 'I'm a thoughtless fool,' the thought came to her that it was better not to make too much of a good thing, so she muttered, 'I'm all right now. It was just a shock.'

'You are not all right, I know the weight of

that damned dog. He's lying with his head well down now; he knows what he's done.'

Poor Bill, she thought, but thank you for the respite. It had been very nice; they must do it again some time. She wanted to laugh, but that would have spoilt it.

As she now raised her eyes to the window, the Captain was looking out and saying under his breath, 'It's our friends; and they're all looking this way. They must be idiots, because it's just after eight and they're making for Breydon now. And the book says one of the better times to cross it is one o'clock tomorrow. The tide is bound to be right out now.'

Sally did not, at this point, enlighten him that some places have two full tides every twenty-four hours, the Thames for instance, something to do with the tide from the Atlantic dividing at Cornwall into two parts, one to go up the west coast of England, round Scotland and down east, the other up the Channel. She had learned this from the shipping talk that went on in her grandmother's kitchen during her childhood.

People on the other boats, she suspected, must be thinking, 'That lot are quite mad to berth near broken stakes with their stern sticking out in the river . . .'

Later, they were actually preparing for bed when the sound of loud voices came over the water. They went out into the cockpit, and from there could see the three cheerful young men, or at least two of them, talking loudly to each other, then shouting down to the third member who must have been still in the cabin, while the boat, at full tilt, made its way towards Breydon Water. This brought from the Captain the exclamation, 'They'll land on a sandbank! You'll see. I'd like to bet that's what the one below is objecting to, crossing at this hour.'

'Well, what about our other friends?'

'Oh, they passed more than an hour ago, and if they keep to the middle of the channel, they'll likely make it. But I myself wouldn't risk it; not when it's getting dark, anyway.'

On this he turned about and went below.

Bill was already tucked up in his blanket; but was not yet on friendly terms with either of his owners. The indignities of the day had been too much for him.

2

The following morning, everything inside the boat was ship-shape and ready for the journey. The tins in the cupboards were all stacked close together; there was no crockery loose anywhere; the gas had been turned off tight; the kettle emptied of its water in case some other boat's heavy wash should shake it from the stove.

Sally pulled on her woollen cap and a short waterproofed coat, because it was still raining, as it had been all night. Then she had realised the necessity for the canvas awning that covered the top of the wheelhouse. But as she made to go up into the cockpit she thought she heard voices and imagined Fred must be talking to someone on the bank. When she emerged it was to see he was in heated conversation with the map and booklet.

'Call themselves cartographers!' he was saying.

'I wonder where this one was when he set out the map, certainly not facing a week on the Broads. And why can't he write plain English?'

His wife could not resist putting in, 'You mean right or left?'

He looked up at her and his tone was very tart as he said, 'No, madam; I don't mean right or left; I mean ebb tide or full tide. What does he mean by slack water?'

She could not miss emitting a 'Huh!' before replying, 'If he says slack water, he means slack water.'

'Oh, does he? Again, madam, what do you know about slack water?'

Sally's tone was now very precise and full of aggravation, as she meant it to be: 'I mean, slack water is a kind of resting period. The ebb tide likes to take its breath before starting out on its return journey; and even when it reaches its height it takes another breath, by the name of slack water, but not so long this time before descending again.'

She now had his full attention. His mouth was slightly agape and his eyes had that dangerous gleam in them when he asked, 'Who, may I ask, informed you of this great piece of nautical wisdom?'

'Oh, I was born to it,' she said. 'Don't forget I came into this world in the north-east, not ten feet from the dock wall at South Shields, and an equal number of yards beyond the wall were a number of berths, where boats tied up when they managed to get into the dock from the North Sea at slack water, or were waiting to leave it. It all depended on which end of the sea was slack at the time to allow them to come up or down the river.'

Last night and his love talk were apparently forgotten, for Fred now banged his fist against the wheel as he said, 'Have you looked at this map?'

'Yes, I have,' she replied politely. 'I have glanced at it.'

'Oh, you have. Then you will have noticed the number of places that this expert tells you you can visit in a week. That is, when you get over Breydon Water. It's equivalent to driving a car from Lands End to John O'Groats without taking the time—' He stopped here; then, as if searching for words, he brought out some which to Sally were surprising: 'To get out for even a pee.'

Fred normally had a great reticence about anything to do with body functions, and that he, the schoolmaster, the exponent of English, should come out with the word 'pee' and not be precise and say 'voiding', seemed hilarious to Sally. She howled with laughter, so much so that she had to turn and go down into the cabin and drop onto the seat until this spasm slowly passed, and Bill stopped scampering around the place as if he, too, were laughing his tail off.

After a long silence above and below deck, she began to feel guilty, and made her way slowly up into the cockpit again.

Fred was sitting there looking utterly dejected, staring over the wheel into the long, rain-swept windscreen.

She stood by his side and, putting her hand on his shoulder, she said softly, 'I'm sorry, Fred. I was being bitchy. I didn't mean it . . . well, not to hurt you.'

When he did not look at her, she turned his face towards her, adding now, 'Please!'

He still did not speak; but what he did touched her more than words: he laid his head on her shoulder. Then, his voice breaking, he muttered, 'It's me. I'm a big-head. I think I know everything; and I can't bear the truth that I don't.'

They finished up with their arms around each

other, with Bill appraising them from the side with a puzzled expression on his face.

By ten o'clock they were out from their berth and in the middle of the river again.

Later, when raising her eyes lazily from the frothing water to roam the reed-waving banks and draw on more practical tags to fit her mood, Sally realised with surprise that the landscape had changed: there were no banks, at least none near enough to be protecting; the river had widened and looked bleak and forbidding; posts, black and dripping green slime, reared up out of the rain-spangled water, which no longer appeared like a river: its width spoke of the sea. She went and stood by her husband, and he, taking his eyes from the windscreen, smiled at her. However, she did not return the smile for there, ahead, for ever ahead it seemed, were posts. On and on they went. In between and around them flowed the black water, with, spreading away from them on either side, mud, the expanses of mud she had seen on the map.

This was Breydon Water.

'It looks frightful,' she said.

'Oh, it's all right,' she was assured.

'How deep will it be?'

'Oh . . .' and he considered. 'Oh . . . now here, it'll be about four feet six.'

To allay her fears, she realised he was making it just deep enough that, should she have to stand in it, her head would be clear.

Sally wanted to believe the lie, but the wide water derided it.

'Why are the posts red on one side and black on the other?'

'Well, I'm not quite sure. I'll have to look it up.'

'Why are they numbered? Look! That one says forty-seven.' She turned and looked back. 'The last one said forty-eight.' Her voice sank. 'Do they go right back to one?'

'Yes; but it doesn't cover all that much distance – three miles or so.'

'Three miles or so of this? Water, mud, and stakes?'

'It's stopped raining,' he said; 'a wind's rising.'

Suddenly she pointed ahead, saying, 'Look! there's a boat on a sandbank. I bet it's those three young men.'

A loud voice came on the wind now, yelling, 'I warned you!' This was from a man approaching the sandbank from their right in a rowing-boat.

As they approached, they saw it was indeed the young men. The biggest of the three was standing at the top of the sandbank laughing his head off. He was obviously drunk. The other two were lower down, their backs against their beached craft; and it was the voice of the quietest one, as Sally thought of him, that now came to them, saying, 'How much longer?' and the answer from the rowing-boat was 'Just about two hours.'

She saw Fred glance quickly towards the map and the guidebook and knew that he was thinking of when he had questioned disdainfully why he should have been advised that the best time for crossing would have been between one and two. And here they were, more than two hours ahead. Yet, as they passed the beached boat, all the man in the rowing-boat did was glance at them, and with a slight shake of his head he turned to the business in hand to answer some question from the quiet man.

Fred said nothing until they were some distance ahead, when Sally remarked, 'The sun's trying to get out,' to which he replied, 'Yes;

and if it stays out I'll take the awning down.'

'How will you manage it on your own?'

'Oh, it's only held to the window frame by three large press-studs.'

Sally looked upwards. The awning was now flapping in the wind, which seemed suddenly to have become quite strong.

'If you like, go down and make some coffee.'

'Oh, no; I'd rather stay here.'

He turned and smiled at her, knowing that she had her own reasons for staying where she was.

Looking ahead, there seemed to be a sight of land. She did not consider the mud on either side as land, not even the apparently firmer banks beyond; yet the faint white blur on the horizon made the distance to it seem greater than when it had been out of sight.

'Look! The sun means to stay,' said Fred quickly. 'You take her; I'll get the awning down. Just hold her steady.'

As Sally took the wheel and watched him climb onto the back of the seat, she said, 'Be careful now.'

He did not answer but went about trying to get the first press-stud out of its socket. It seemed to be taking much effort; but then, once it was free, the end of the awning flapped its release wildly.

Fred was now tugging at the middle stud, which, fortunately, came away much more easily; but now the wildly flapping canvas awning was obscuring him from her view. She could hear, though, that he was having further difficulty with the third stud.

Then it all happened suddenly. Fred seemed to have shot into the air and had disappeared.

She screamed, and jumped from the wheel to gaze at where the awning, acting like a roller blind, had returned neatly to its bed in the lip overhanging the cabin top, which she could now see in its entirety.

There was no sign of Fred. Oh, God! Had he been shot over the top and into that filthy mud behind, in which case he was probably dead at this minute?

Sally jumped back to the wheel and shut off the engine. As she felt the craft begin to move out of control, a weak voice, coming out of the air, yelled, 'Get back to the wheel and start her. And stay there!'

She looked down to Bill, to discover that he was lying in the far corner of the cockpit, huddled against her husband's crumpled body.

As she made to jump up again, a low but firm voice said, 'Stay where you are. Keep her straight.'

Trembling from head to foot, she looked to where he was now unwinding his legs from beneath him, then feeling them to see whether or not they were broken.

She was awed when he did not attempt to stand up, but came towards her on his hands and knees. Then, slowly pulling himself up on-to one of the cockpit seats, he gasped for a moment or two before putting his hand on the wheel and saying, 'Get me a strong coffee, and bring a pillow.'

Sally did not question his command, only saw him bend forward and bring his other hand on to the wheel. She dashed below.

Never in her life had she moved so quickly. It took her about three minutes to make hot strong coffee and return with it and the pillow to the deck.

In amazement, she watched him swallow the coffee in two long gulps; afterwards he directed her to put the pillow at his back.

Then he said, 'Bring the brandy flask.'

Again he amazed her by emptying the cap of brandy at one gulp; then refilling it and sending that down after the first lot.

He did not attempt to get on the seat in front of the wheel, but kneeling sideways on the pillow, he said, 'Take her and keep her steady.'

With shaking hands, Sally did what she had been told to do.

When he groaned once or twice, she did not turn towards him to ask how he felt: he had been hurt somewhere, and badly, else he would not have been acting like this.

It was some time before he next spoke.

'When we are nearing Yarmouth,' he said, 'turn left – when I tell you, mind. Then make for the yacht bay.'

The next half-hour was like a terrifying dream. But then there she was, waking up to the fact that there were two sailing boats leaving their mooring and that she had slowed down to a crawl, waiting for them to clear it before slipping slowly into their place at the quay.

Automatically now, as if driven by some inward knowledge, she turned off the engine, jumped out and fastened both ends of *Dogfish Three* to the rings on the quayside.

This done, she let out a low breath, then saw Fred pull himself slowly up from his seat and, almost doubled up, make his way down to the cabin. She noticed that Bill had followed him instead of standing waiting to be pulled onto the land that was now so close.

When she reached the cabin, Fred was trying to lift his legs up onto the seat where he could lie back.

In a minute she had settled him, then said, 'What is it, darling? Where are you hurt?'

He muttered, 'Nowhere, really; just shaken. And my head aches.'

He put his hand towards the back of his head; and when she felt his scalp, she exclaimed, 'Oh, good gracious! Oh, darling. You say you're not hurt . . .'

The lump under her hand was bigger than . . . the only description that came was a large duck-egg.

'You must see a doctor.'

'No! No.' His tone was emphatic. 'It's only a bump, and my back feels a little sore.'

Sally straightened up. He *should* see a doctor; but she'd leave it for this afternoon; perhaps after a sleep he might feel better.

She went into the galley and opened the door into the stern well; and there, standing in *his* stern well, was, to her further amazement and not a little annoyance, the youth of *Dogfish*

Two. He was staring at her with the same look his father had earlier bestowed.

But what did it matter? She turned about and went back into the galley and started to prepare the lunch, which she doubted Fred would eat.

As she had surmised, he could not eat anything; but he drank three cups of tea, before asking for two aspirins.

At this request she hesitated before saying, 'I don't think you should have aspirins now; you've had quite a lot of brandy.'

'What does it matter?' he said dully. 'It's a pain-killer, and I want that now.'

'It's a doctor you want.'

'No! No; I tell you, no.'

The rest of that day, and the day that followed, was a bad memory, except for one incident that would perhaps at another time have been funny and given them a good laugh.

Sally had said, 'I must take Bill out. The poor fellow is bursting again, and he's been so good about waiting – he knows you aren't well. I'll not be long ... You'll not try to move, will you?'

He managed a weak smile as he said, 'Unfortunately, there's no fear of that ...'

There were a number of people busy cleaning their boats, and these she passed without incident; but there, before her, strolling leisurely along, were the occupants of *Dogfish One*. Between the man and woman trotted their bulging-eyed, plain-faced little dog. Her master held her lead as she held Bill's. Then, with lightning speed, the little animal ran behind her mistress, darted through her legs, over her foot and within sniffing distance of Bill. He, amazingly, seemed not a bit surprised, but received her kiss, then returned it, with interest: a great sloppy lick over her entire face.

Talk about love at first sight, or the love-meeting after years of separation! The last time these two had faced each other had been amidst a series of growls, barks and snarls through windscreens.

It would appear that the owners of the lovers had been struck quite dumb for some seconds.

Then the lady whipped up her beloved pet, away from this horrible brute, and Sally hauled Bill further onto the path. She could only mutter, 'I'm sorry. I'm sorry.' Yet, as she pulled him along to an open place of land she was asking herself, Why was I sorry? He hadn't made the first move. Oh, if Fred had only been well! How he would have laughed at this . . .

When, later in the day, she again took Bill out, it was at the end of a very short lead. And on the following day, too. It was about four o'clock in the afternoon – his second outing of the day – when, nearing the clearing, a voice from behind said to her, 'Excuse me, but I must tell you I was witness to the love scene of yesterday.' The young man pointed to Bill. 'It was very funny. Heloïse and Abelard all over again.'

Sally looked at the third member of the noisy threesome, the quiet one, as she thought of him, and she smiled and said, 'It was funny, wasn't it?'

'I saw your boat passing yesterday when we were stuck on the sandbank.'

'That must have been a nasty experience.'

'It's the first time it's happened to me,' he said. 'I used to cross Breydon often some years ago. But Big Charles' – he paused, then laughed – 'the one who you will have noticed makes the most noise every time he opens his mouth, would have us do a little weaving. You saw the result . . . Is your husband not well?'

'No; I'm sorry to say he had an accident on board.'

'Is it bad?'

'I don't really know. I only know he's not

well. It's so unlike him to lie still; he's such a live wire.'

'So I understand from your neighbour. You had a little *contretemps* back in the bay. Is he a teacher of Latin?'

'No; he's a maths master, but well versed in Latin,' Sally said proudly.

He laughed again, saying, 'So I was given to understand. Apparently he didn't expect Horace to be understood. When the youngster on board came back at him, literally with chapter and verse, "I abhor the unhallowed mob and hold it aloof," it must have shaken him a bit: from their Mancunian accents he hadn't expected that.'

Her voice stiff, Sally said, 'You seem to have learned a lot about us in a very short time.'

'Oh, please don't be annoyed, because it pleased me yet again to know that one should never go on face values. You see, that neighbour of yours turned out to be a very thoughtful individual. On first acquaintance, I wasn't taken with him myself. But not seeing your husband out and about, and you having to take the dog out, and his wife, glimpsing you in the bows looking very distressed, thought there must be something wrong . . .'

Oh, dear God! That was the night of the

accident when she had sat crying. Fred had gone to sleep. He had eaten nothing all day, and still he wouldn't let her call a doctor, or look at his back.

'Now what did our gentleman from Manchester do? It would appear that his boat being next to ours he heard Big Charlie and Peter arguing, and Charlie referring to Peter as a doctor who thought he knew everything. So he came to me and said that he thought you must be worried about your husband, and if my friend was really a doctor perhaps he could talk to him. So please don't be annoyed when I say that Peter has gone along to your boat now and gatecrashed in. I'd give him a few more minutes before you return. Now don't worry; he's a very tactful fellow.'

To say she was amazed was putting it mildly, not only where the three young men were concerned, but also by the fact that their hated neighbour had shown so much feeling. As this man had said, one should not go on face values ... Well, one lived and learned, if one was sensible.

'Are you a doctor too?'

'No.' He gave a gurgle of a laugh. 'I'm a budding priest. Parson would be the ordinary name for it. I've never been able to see why the Catholic clergy can be dubbed priests, but Protestants, although on the same road, are generally known as parsons.'

Sally had nothing to say; actually she was dumbfounded. Here was this fellow who was wearing the oldest-looking pullover she had ever seen and a pair of patched trousers, his feet bare except for a pair of open-toed sandals, saying he was studying for the priesthood.

She heard herself ask, 'Where do you think your parish will be?' She was imagining somewhere in a middle-class area, when he amazed her further by saying, 'As near my father's as possible, in the East End of London.'

She looked at him blankly, then managed to mutter, 'It's as you said a while ago, one lives and learns. Now, I'd better get back, don't you think?'

'Yes, of course. The introductions will be over by now. And talking of introductions, my name's James Watson.'

Before he moved away, he bent and patted Bill's head, saying, 'He's a splendid-looking fellow. My mother has a bulldog. She thinks she's wonderful, but now she slavers all the time and snores. She's thirteen years old.'

All she could do was nod at him and smile.

Before she stepped into *Dogfish Three* she held up a finger in warning to Bill, and said, with authority, 'Quiet now! Quiet!'

She stepped over the gunwale and onto the seat without rocking the boat. When Bill stood beside her she led him to his usual corner on the leather seat and fixed his lead round one of the canopy posts, so that he could not jump down; then moved quietly to the steps leading into the cabin, and listened to a voice saying, 'Good Lord!' which had a laugh behind it. 'If you made a slight slit in that and laced it up, you'd have a miniature football . . . Pains badly?'

'Not so much as my neck.'

'Yes; that's bound to be affected by it. Well, as I said, you have a bad case of concussion. And, as you know, the only cure for that is rest for two or three days. Well, if they yank you off to hospital, it could be longer, you know. How's the back?'

There was a long pause before she heard Fred say, 'Pretty sore.'

'We'd better have a look at it, then.'

At this point, Sally thought she should make her appearance, for, once that pyjama jacket was put back on again, she had a suspicion she wouldn't be given the chance to see the damage to his back.

'Oh! Hello there, Mrs Carpenter. Believe it or not, I'm a doctor. Peter Wheeler, one of the mad hatters from the beached craft. Your husband has had a very nasty fall; I'm about to have a look at his back. Perhaps you'll help me off with his pyjama coat.'

As yet, she hadn't opened her mouth. That was until she had gently eased Fred out of one sleeve of his pyjamas, when it was almost a shout she emitted: 'Oh, my God! What have you done to your back?'

From his shoulders down to the top of his buttocks he was black and blue.

The doctor's voice now said quietly, 'Indeed, my God!'

He looked at Fred's ashen face. 'No wonder you haven't wanted to move. And there are two places that definitely need a pad with a rubber covering. I'm sorry, man, but I say again, you should be in hospital . . . Your wife'll be all right. We'll be staying here, and could give her a hand if she needs it.'

'No. No; I told you.'

The young man turned to Sally, saying,

'Would you get me a bowl of boiled water, Mrs Carpenter, please?'

She scrambled to do his bidding, then watched him go to the other seat and take from his black bag a small bottle, and pour half of its contents into the water.

After putting on a pair of rubber gloves, he split open a plastic bag, and took from it a sponge and dropped it into the bowl. Then he asked for a towel, and indicated she tuck it under Fred, who was now lying on his side.

Silently she watched the young man dabbing the sponge all over her husband's back, and saying, 'That should soothe it for a time. I'm not going to dry it, it'll do that itself. But I shall put some salve on those grazes. It might sting a bit. Then I'll put that rubber pad on; it'll keep it clean for a few days. What should happen now' – he had turned to Sally – 'is that he should be put to bed. But then you would be unable to get about the cabin. So what I suggest is, you take away those cushions' – he pointed to the back of the seat – 'that'll give you more room. Your bed tick is thin enough to be doubled. He'll be more comfortable and you can get past.'

'She'll never be able to do that on her own.'

'Don't worry, Mr Carpenter. Just don't

worry. James and I will come along and fix things. We used these little craft often years ago in our vacs.' Then he added, 'How does the back feel now?'

'Oh, much easier. Thank you . . . This is all very kind of you, you know.'

'Not at all. Not at all. We are glad, in a way. It gets us rid of Pontoon Mouth. He's the big fellow. We'll tell you about him later; there's quite a story there.'

Sally followed the surprising doctor up into the wheelhouse; and there whispered, 'I just don't know how to thank you. I've been worried to death. He should be in hospital, I know; but you can see he's so stubborn.'

The doctor laughed gently, then said, 'Yes; and you're the reason for it,' with which enigmatic reply he stepped off the boat.

They had arrived at Oulton Broad Yacht Station on the Saturday; on the Sunday they had crossed Breydon Water, where the accident happened; Sally spent Monday going crazy with worry over what had happened to Fred, and his reactions to it; that afternoon she had her first conversation with James Watson, followed by the meeting with Peter Wheeler, who unveiled the horror of Fred's back and the awful fact that he was suffering from concussion and needed rest if he were to recover sufficiently to get them home.

She need not have worried. Apparently, it was all settled. The following morning, Tuesday, they had another visit from Dr Wheeler, accompanied by his friend.

They rearranged the cabin and then sat looking at Fred. It was James Watson who said, 'You're going to be bed-bound, Mr Carpenter, for the next couple of days, so I understand, and it won't be pleasant for either of you tied up to this quay with all the coming and going and the bustle and noise around you; so we have a suggestion.

'It's like this. During the years we have spent on these rivers there was a part we called our secret slipway. It led nowhere; but it was so peaceful, with a good view across green farming land. And so, this morning, as we were making for there ourselves, hoping to get Pontoon Mouth to sober up, we thought that you might like us to lead you up there, where you could lie in peace for the next two days, before you return across Breydon Water again on Friday, ready to slip back into Oulton Broad Yacht Station on Saturday morning.

'We have to leave on Friday, for I must be back at college on Monday. Peter here, too, will have a queue of patients waiting for him at home. What do you think?'

'It's very kind of you,' said Fred. 'And I'm not in any position at the moment to make any plans, am I? What do you think, dear?' He had turned to Sally.

'It sounds lovely,' she said. 'But we'll need provisions quite soon.'

'Don't worry about that,' put in the young doctor quickly. 'We're taking the boat straight back to Yarmouth today after we leave you, in order to catch the train to London, because we have an appointment with James's father. We'll be back on Thursday morning, and there are one or two nice corner shops up there. One is called Harrods.'

Sally laughed. 'Yes, with everything three times the price.'

'Oh, yes,' said the doctor, himself laughing now; 'but isn't it a nice feeling walking along the street swinging a bag with Harrods printed on it in large letters? Anyway, we'll be passing you in a few minutes, and we'll slip you a bottle of milk we have spare, and you slip us a shopping

list. Get her ready now for off and follow us.'
He turned to Fred and said, 'How are you
feeling now, sir?'

'Better, thank you. Oh, much better.'

'Your back still aching?'

'Oh, not so bad at all, thanks to you.'

'That's good. Well, we'll leave things as they
are till we get back. We must be off now.'

In the cockpit, he said to Sally, 'You'll be able
to manage her?'

'Oh, yes. Yes. After that journey through
Breydon I think I could take a steamer across the
Channel now.'

She and Fred both laughed, and James added,
'Good girl!'

After they were gone, she stood for a moment
thinking. They were lovely, like two fathers
looking after Fred and herself. Even if she was
in her early forties, and Fred six years younger.
Fathers indeed!

That Tuesday morning, they moved from the
yacht station. Sally endeavoured to keep her
eyes on the boat ahead so did not take in the
places they were passing.

Soon James Watson was signalling her to

slow down. He pointed to his right and shouted, 'The next cut on the left,' then added, 'Can you whistle?'

'Whistle?' she shouted back. 'Yes, I can whistle.'

'Well, when you reach a green bank, tie up and whistle. That's if you feel it's all right.'

She did as she had been directed, and went through a green channel into an open space where the bank was almost on a level with the gunwale. Quickly, she shut off the engine, jumped out, thrust in the rond anchors, then whistled shrilly, to be answered by the toot-toot of a horn.

She went downstairs and said to her smiling husband, 'We're all set, but I'll see to the oil and things first.'

'Good girl!' he said. 'You've done marvellously.'

Ten minutes later, Sally slumped on his makeshift bed and said, 'It's lovely here. You can see for miles over the far bank; it's a little lower that side. Perhaps tomorrow you'll be able to sit outside in the cockpit.'

He reached out and said, 'Give me your hand.' He stroked it, and his voice was soft as he said, 'You're not only beautiful, but you're charming, for you have charmed two of your noisy young men.'

'Charmed!' she said indignantly. 'A doctor and a priest just doing their duty because the opportunity occurred? Now, let's be practical: are you hungry?'

'It's funny, but I am a little.'

'Well, it's not funny, I am a lot, I mean hungry. What about bacon and eggs, fried bread and a sausage?'

'Oh!' he laughed. 'You've forgotten the kidney.'

'Well,' she rose, laughing herself now, 'if those two fellows go to Harrods, we'll likely have them on Thursday. But seriously, they are nice chaps, aren't they?'

'Yes, they are. And to think we owe them to the kind concern of our Mancunian friends . . .'

It was a wonderful day. The sun came out, really hot at times. Bill thought he had reached his seventh heaven for, after a thorough search of the land surrounding this wired-in field, Sally let him off the lead. He romped for a time, and explored, but then returned to the boat; in spite of his freedom, it would seem he did not want to be separated from his owners.

The next day, she banked Fred up on the bed

so that he could see further out of the window; then she pushed a stool near him and asked, 'Are you really feeling better?'

'Oh, much,' he replied. 'And I'll get up tomorrow and do a little walking. It looks lovely out there; I could stay here for a week. I can't believe it's Wednesday already, and we must be back in dock by Friday night.'

He turned towards her and said, 'I wonder what the boys are doing in London.'

'I do too. But I bet they'll not be back till late tomorrow, with Pontoon Mouth singing his head off.'

She was wrong there, for shortly after midday the next day, there they were sailing past and calling out, 'Be with you shortly!'

'No roaring . . . no singing,' said Fred. 'They must have left him behind.'

'We'll soon know.'

It wasn't ten minutes later when they entered the cabin, and Fred watched Peter hand Sally a bag with 'Harrods' printed across it, at which they all burst out laughing.

'I told you there was a good corner shop up there. See if we've brought everything you want.'

She turned out the contents of the heavy

bag, and exclaimed, 'Oh, Peter! You shouldn't.'

'It was half-price day,' he said.

Apart from the bread, tea, sugar, butter and ham she had asked for, there were tins of fruit, pots of dressed crab and pâté, special marmalade, two tins of treacle pudding, a box of chocolates, and another of almonds and raisins.

She wanted to turn and fling her arms around them; instead she looked at Fred and asked, 'What can we say to this?' And he, looking at their benefactors, said, 'Only thank you, fellows, very much indeed. You're placing us more and more in your debt.'

'Nonsense! Nonsense!' said Peter. 'But aren't you going to ask what we've done to Pontoon Mouth, and why we went to London?'

Fred laughed. 'To tell you the truth, we just can't wait to find out.'

'Well, let's get settled and we'll tell you a story. That's after we have a glass of this.' Peter pulled from his jacket pocket a bottle of muscat, saying, 'It's an either-sex drink, and it's very nice.'

With this, he uncorked the bottle, took four small glass mugs from the rack and filled each with wine. Then they all held them up together as he said, 'To new but definitely future friends.'

Following this, they settled down round the bed.

It was Peter who looked at James and said, 'You're the Bible-pusher and fable-spouter, so I leave you to tell the tale.'

James laughed and said, 'Well, before I begin I'll say we won't be having the company of our friend for some time. He was to meet us off the train this morning. He hadn't returned to the boat. So we guessed he had found a new lady-love, and that we wouldn't see him again until we went back to dock tomorrow. Tomorrow is our last day, and we had arranged to have a little farewell do before parting on our several ways: Peter back to his patients; me to college; and Big Charlie McHannen to America. The latest news from there his valet-cum-warder imparted to us yesterday: America is too hot to hold him.

'Now, we'll go back to the beginning. As I understand it, Charlie's great-grandfather came over from Ireland in the middle of the last century in one of the starving boats. And even as a child, he understood that without money his father and family might die. He seemed to be the only one of the line with an astute mind, for he did not bother to beg, instead he stole.

In between times he took every job available to him, from sweeping the streets to making matchboxes at slave-labour rates; to running for a betting business; to setting one up on his own, no bet higher than sixpence, which within ten years and studying the *Financial Times* introduced him to the stock market. He was a gambler and would risk anything, even take on a rotting business, going on the premise that even rotting apples could make a certain kind of cider.

'He didn't marry until he was forty; then he had a son and brought him up on the same lines along which he himself had travelled, but in a more polished fashion.

'His son, though not blessed with brains, was a good imitator. He married and had a son, Mike.

'By now, Mike's father and grandfather were sharing a company. One of them only had to find a rotten hulk of a boat, employ some of the still starving Irish who were willing to work for bread and beer, and another small cargo boat was added to the McHannen fleet.

'It was soon after the First World War that this young Mike McHannen went to America, set up in business, married and had a son.

'He had picked his wife with the knowledge that her father, too, was well up in the business field and with a good head on his shoulders. From this marriage was born our friend, Charles McHannen, and from the moment of his first yell, it would seem he never stopped. He had only to yell to get someone to do his bidding and give him whatever he wanted.

'He was six years old when his mother felt she had had enough of both him and his father and walked out on them.

'Up till then, young Charles had been fed with a silver spoon; but from that moment his father turned it into a gold one. Everything he wanted he got; nothing he did was wrong. It was all put down to his being a braw Irish laddie. That was until he became engaged to the daughter of one of his father's partners. She was a high-spirited society beauty. The wedding arranged matched anything our royalty here could put on: all New York who was anybody was invited. Then bang! A fortnight before the appointed date the spirited lady came to him, threw her engagement ring into the fire, and then, I understand, to use her own words, which the headlines of the papers quoted, she told him where he could go and take his two fancy women with him.

'The newspapers, as you can imagine, had a field day.

'The next piece of news was that her father confronted the great Mike McHannen and told him exactly what he thought of him; and McHannen told him that if he didn't see that his daughter took back her words and continue with the wedding arrangements, and not make a laughing-stock out of him, he would ruin him.

'By this time most of New York was well into the picture, and Big Charlie couldn't stand it, so fled to England. And who do you think he came to? To Peter, there. He and I were the only two friends he had previously made in this country, during his university days here. And Peter's father being a doctor, and Peter himself one, what could they do for him? He was in a hellish state.

'Peter's father, being a naturally kind man, suggested that Peter and I, having arranged for a trip on the Broads while Peter's wife Gail had gone to visit her parents in Scotland, should take him along with us.'

James paused here and took a deep breath before going on: 'Well, you've seen and heard what we took on, haven't you? And, on the quiet, we've talked about what he's likely to do with himself after we leave him. It isn't all his fault, you know, that he's turned out like this: his whole childhood was ruined through lack of proper care and through being hopelessly over-indulged. He's never known what it is to have wanted anything and not be given it. So Peter, here, thought up a crazy plan; which is really why we rushed to London on Tuesday to put it to my father. It's just this. You see, Charles can drink most men under the table and still stand on his feet and go on singing. But now and again, as we had previously discovered during the two years we knew him, there comes a point when he blots right out. It's usually after mixing his drinks, whisky and rum, which is followed by a dreadful two-day hangover, when he can hardly move for the pain in his head.'

At this point, Peter started to laugh as he said, 'I could see it all happening, for, as James's father said, it was being worked by two healers of the body and one of the soul.'

He laughed again, then said, 'Go on now, James, and tell them the plot.'

'We intend to get him dead drunk,' said James, 'drop him in the gutter here and there to muddy his clothes, get him into Father's old banger and take him deep into the East End to a parishioner friend of my father, Joseph Connolly, who has fallen in with the plan, and leave him there.' And here, he lay back against the window and ended, 'Well, that's about it. We'll know nothing more until my father writes and informs us how it's going. We only hope it shows Big-mouth how the other half of the world lives, and take it from there. Anyway,' he said, 'when he does I'll give you a ring.' He paused before he added, 'That's if you would like to keep in touch.'

Fred was before Sally in answering, 'Oh, yes; yes, by all means do let us know.

'Do you think he'll turn up at Oulton tomorrow looking for you?' he continued.

'Oh, yes; of course he will. We have already arranged a farewell dinner for tomorrow night. What happens to him afterwards is in the lap of the gods, or the Connollys, and, of course, James's father, who is a rare old schemer for the saving of souls.

'Anyway, about you two.' Peter looked from Sally to Fred. 'As you know, we give up our boat tomorrow. Now, it's difficult getting out of this retreat because one has to back out, so we think we should take you with us earlier in the morning and see you settled in a nice little creek we know of, close to Breydon Water. You can lie there until high tide and get across Breydon and into Oulton Broad by Friday night. It'll be straight going from there. What about it?'

'Oh, that suits us,' said Fred; 'and I'll be on my feet tomorrow.'

'You might be,' put in Peter; 'but you must still be careful. That back of yours will take a week or so to heal.'

So it was left at this, except that Sally's last words were, 'I'll be sorry to leave here, it's so beautiful.'

3

The next morning everything was plain sailing. They left the haven without a hitch, and for the next hour followed their friends.

It was about ten o'clock when James, in the stern well ahead, raised an arm pointing to the right, and indicating Sally should slow down.

She followed this instruction, Fred sitting in the seat by her side.

Their friends soon turned into a cut, and just as she was about to follow them, she noticed to her horror that straight ahead there were four sailing boats ready to come out, one apparently aiming straight at the left of *Dogfish Three*. To Sally's amazement she saw a young woman sitting calmly outside a low cabin on it suckling a baby.

In a lightning move, she turned slightly to her right, and the yacht slid by.

But now, down on her right, another was coming at them, and too close for comfort, so she swung back to the left. It cleared within inches, and was followed by another which bumped them slightly as they passed, the man at the wheel emitting a high noise, whether of triumph or defeat, Sally didn't know.

Then, at the sight now before her, it was Fred who uttered a cry: 'I'll take her.'

Sally bawled at him, 'No!', for the large sailing vessel was headed straight for their bow. If she remained on course, he would crash into them: her only recourse was to reverse, but how? How she found the knob that did the trick, she didn't know, but there was a grinding beneath their feet, which meant that the propeller was answering her command; *Dogfish Three* moved at least six inches back, and at that moment Sally knew that if the windscreen had been open she could have leaned forward and grabbed the fellow's sail; so close was his craft to them.

When he was past and she could see ahead, James Watson was standing on the gunwale of his boat, his face full of concern and wonder.

Behind them, there was a great deal of noise, and Fred, putting his hand on the wheel, in a shaking voice said, 'Look round.'

Sally bent sideways and looked along the cabin side, and there were the four sailing vessels all seemingly lined up and their crews waving, and one of them yelled, 'Well done! Splendid!' Another followed with 'Join us at any time!'

As Sally turned back to the wheel, Fred put his hand on her shoulder. His face looked rather white but he was smiling and his eyes spoke volumes; he did not say a word.

She could honestly say that was the proudest moment in her life: she was admiral of the fleet. Her flotilla had passed her without a scratch. It was the kind of triumph experienced only once in a lifetime.

She followed James and Peter up the creek, until James indicated a berth next to what appeared to be an eight-to-ten-berth cruiser. Immediately she could see the reason for this: it would be easier for them to get out later if they berthed below *Dogfish Three*.

Both craft were tied up when Peter and James came hurrying to them and dropped into the wheelhouse. It was Peter who said, 'Lady, that's the best piece of manoeuvring I've seen on these waters,' and turning to Fred, he said, 'Wasn't she marvellous?'

'No more than usual,' replied Fred gallantly; 'only, mind, I was a little nervous when that last fellow came head on at her.'

'Nervous?' cried James now. 'My hair was standing on end!'

Suddenly they all turned to where some argument appeared to have started on the towpath. Coming towards them were two young girls with a baby in a pushchair. The child was yelling its head off; that was, until one of the girls pushed a dummy into its mouth. She looked about fifteen; she had short black hair and a round pert face with a snub nose. Her companion's head was a mass of permed curls, and she was saying, 'You shouldn't do that. If Ella finds out she'll go mad. The book says it's wrong to give them dummies.'

The answer she was given by the short-haired girl in a raucous voice was, 'Bugger Ella and the dummy! And you, Lucy, an' all. If you go and tell her I keep one in my pocket, I'll scalp you and your bunch of frizz.'

A shout from the cockpit startled them all, for Peter had called out, 'Rosie! It is, isn't it, Rosie?'

'Eeh, by!' The dark-haired girl turned to Peter who was leaning over the gunwale, his hand outstretched. 'What are you doing here?

'And you an' all, Mr Watson.' She was addressing James, who was also holding out a hand to her.

'It was last Saturday night, wasn't it?' she was saying. 'I've thought about you two a lot since, and Whalemouth. Is he here, an' all?'

'No; he's staying with friends in London.'

'Thank God for that.'

'You went off him, didn't you, Rosie?' Peter said.

'Off him! You should have heard what I said to him.'

A voice crying, 'Rosie!' boomed over them, and she looked back to the deck of the high cruiser, and shouted at the young woman standing there, 'All right! We'll take him for his run. Why don't you do it yourself for a change? He's your baby.'

'Don't you give me any mouth; I'll tell your ma.'

'Tell her what the hell you like; and you can both go for a walk there, and take your time.'

'Eeh, Rosie! Rosie. You'll get it in the neck.' This last came from Miss Frizzy-head.

James and Peter were shaking with laughter, and Peter said, 'Look, Rosie, slip along later. We'd love to have a crack. But make it soon because we must be off. Our friends here will be staying till late this afternoon. We'll make the introductions later. But go on, now, and get your dummy walk over; else I can see you being locked in.'

'Oh, that won't be the first time,' said Rosie. 'They've tried it before.'

The four returned to the cabin of *Dogfish Three*, and Sally said to Peter, 'You know her?'

'I feel I've known her for years, but we met for the first time on Saturday night. We had got away early in the afternoon and stopped at a place near Acle. We had a meal and sat around listening to Pontoon Mouth's latest history while he slugged back whisky like water.

'We had decided to stay there for the night when this very large motor cruiser moored alongside us, and the whole crew, all ten of them, spilled into the bar.

'They were definitely from Birmingham. What we noticed was the hair-do of three of the women. They were all about the same height, but the biggest-made one looked as though she had a mop of permed blond wire. The hair of another, younger, one was dyed bright red; the third was a perm of grey and white.

'My first impression was of three witches;

and, when she opened her coat, I saw to my amazement the big one was wearing an old-fashioned bib pinny.

'The red-headed younger woman of about twenty was carrying a child – you saw her just now. Then there were also two girls, one of whom I took to be fifteen or sixteen, with short-cropped black hair; the other, slightly younger, had permed curls down to her neck.

'The youngest male was a boy of about thirteen.

'The three men stood together at one end of the bar, the women, except for the short-haired girl, were grouped at the other end, some sitting on forms along a wall.

'The short-haired girl was walking down the room, and as I passed her when I was carrying two lagers back to our table I must have nudged her.

'She turned on me quickly and I said, "Oh, I am sorry. I hope I haven't spilled any on you."

'For a moment she looked at me; then in a broad Birmingham twang, she said, "It could only have improved it if you had. Take something to spoil this rig-out."

'Being gallant, I now replied, "Oh, you look very nice," but then was amazed at her retort:

"The hell I do! And I know it. So don't waste your nice words on me."

'I began to laugh and she said, "Look! You're spilling your beer." Then I dared to say to her, "Come and sit down for a moment," and practically collapsed when she answered, "What! Come and sit down with you? Do you want to see a bloody riot?" – she jerked her head back to the female members of her family sitting in a corner – "Those three Amazons – me auntie, me mum and me cousin – would lynch you."

'I glanced back at the three women now staring towards us, and she did too. Then I almost did drop the lager when she said, "Oh, what the hell! Come on; where're you sitting?"

'I cannot begin to put into conversation form what followed. We laughed as we haven't done for years, didn't we?'

James said, 'Indeed we did. We had never come across her like. She was a one-off. And everything was running smoothly until our friend appeared and joined us. His new lady-friend whom he had picked up earlier that evening must have had more than enough of him, because we saw her leave the inn by herself. Of course, Pontoon Mouth could only glare at our new acquaintance, at least for the first few moments, and that we seemed to have picked up with such a plain and nondescript individual had kept him silent for the longest period since he had first joined us for the holiday. And when he spoke, it was to ask the question we should have asked earlier on. And she, too, looked at him silently before she answered, "Rosie Stevenson; what's yours?"

' "Oh, mine, I'm Charles Victor McHannen."

'The reply he received startled him: "Well, you're none the better for that."

'It was now that one of the witches, the blonde one, her mother, passed us. She did not cast her eyes in our direction, but she said one word only, and there was deep meaning in it, "Ro-sie!"

'But Rosie did not turn her head. She looked from me to Peter here and said, "It's been nice talking to you."

' "And to you, Rosie," we both answered.

'At this she got up and followed the blond-haired woman down the passage which led to the ladies'.

'I said, "It's about time we were getting aboard and settling down, eh? It's been a long day."

'We placed our mugs on the counter and were

thanking the landlady when we heard a yell and a high screech and someone jabbering at the top of their voice.

'We looked back at our table. Pontoon Mouth wasn't there.

'When we reached the passage, we saw what the commotion was about. Two men, one elderly, one young, were pulling Rosie away from our whisky-sodden friend who was leaning back against a wall, one hand placed across the front of his trousers, the other cupping his cheek, and the elderly man turned on me and bawled, "You'd better get your friend aboard your boat while he's still able to walk."

'We asked no more questions, but hauled Pontoon from the wall and to the boat and threw him fully clothed onto a back bunk; and Peter warned, "Move from there if you dare. I'll throw you overboard. I swear to God I will."

'Although it was getting dusk, we started the engine, cast off, and made our way back over Breydon, intending to go into dock the next morning and curtail the trip. But he woke up full of apologies, even if not completely sober, and begged us to go on as we had originally planned.

'And so we again made our way back to Breydon. Of course, by now we hadn't taken the tides into account. So that's where you saw us, stuck on the mud.'

The sound of voices, seeming to come from *Dogfish Three*'s wheelhouse, startled them all for a moment until Sally said, 'They must be having a to-do next door.'

Then quite clearly they heard a man's voice say, 'If she wants to go and talk with the fellas, she can go and have a talk with them. And it's me that's saying it . . . You say she's getting beyond herself. Well, all I can say is, it's about time she did. What has she to gain among your lot? Once it used to be, she's breaking up the family, stepping out of her place. But where's the family gone now? As far away from you as they can get. And what have we got? All your damn nieces and nephews, all on the scrounge, or asking for loans that they never pay back.'

A female voice came now: 'They're all I've got. As for her, she's going into the factory as soon as she leaves that school. I'll see to that if it's the last thing I do.'

'It likely will be.'

A new voice joined in, saying, 'Shut that

bloody door. D'you want the whole river to know your business?'

The voices still continued, but now faintly, and Sally turned and looked from one to the other. It was James who spoke, saying, 'Poor Rosie.'

'Well, there's one thing,' Fred put in: 'that seemed to be her father talking. And he's certainly for her. Anyway, I bet she'll be along in a minute.'

'Yes,' said Peter; 'I bet she will. I'll bring her in here . . . may we?' to which Sally answered on a laugh, 'I'm dying to hear more from Rosie.'

It was more than fifteen minutes later and Rosie was about to pass *Dogfish Three* on her way to the boys' boat, as Sally still thought of them, when a hiss from Peter and his hand outstretched brought her over the gunwale and down the steps into the cabin, where she immediately bent down to Bill and, patting his head, said, 'Hello, old fellow! What's your name?'

'Bill,' Sally said.

'We have a dog back home,' said Rosie. 'He's a mongrel – Heinz fifty-seven varieties – he's called Stinker. He's been left with me granny. And I know the poor fella will be kept tied up in the yard. He hates me granny, that's me mother's mother. And he's not the only one.'

'Sit down,' Sally said, 'if you can squeeze in; and as your friends don't seem to be about to introduce us, I shall. This one' – she pointed to Fred – 'sitting pale and weary-looking is my husband Fred. He has a very bad back, brought about by attempting to fly over Breydon Water.'

Rosie looked at Fred and laughed as she said, 'Why didn't you just swim?' and he answered her, 'Because I'm a big-head, Rosie, and I've always wanted to fly. My doctor here' – he pointed to Peter – 'will tell you all about it.'

Looking at Rosie, Peter said, 'You've been having a shindy next door. We couldn't help overhearing.'

'Oh, that was nothing; just a practice do,' she said. 'Look at me!' And she looked from one to the other. 'Can you see me stepping out of me place, when it's written all over me, and I just have to open me mouth and it comes out in headlines? It's all because I found out there are different people in the world, besides me mum's stinking family, who haven't a penn'orth of brains between them, and so she queens it over them – "Go to Aunt Florrie, she knows," or "Go to Aunt Florrie, she'll help you out," or "She'll make him do it." Well, she found out some time ago that I could see through her. Her and her pinnies! Believe it or not, she goes to our factory with that pinny on, just to prove to them, she says, that she's not getting above herself and doesn't need any fancy clothes.'

'You have a factory, then?' said Peter.

'Yes; and fifty machinists in it. She was one of them at one time.'

'What d'you make?' he asked.

'Oh, all kinds,' said Rosie. 'Cheapish things. No fancy goods. Dad goes up to London three days a week, and picks the cloth and such. But really that's just an excuse; he goes to visit Gran, his mother. He has a good manager, a Mr Jackson. Me mum hates him, because he knows all about her; and he loathes her. He wants to improve the style of things; she's all for keeping to pinnies and aprons, and the plainest of frocks. Well,' she looked at Peter and laughed as she said, 'as I told you, you couldn't spoil that one I had on the other night when you thought you had spilt the beer over it.'

'Oh, about Saturday night,' James said. 'What happened around the corner to make all that hubbub?'

'Well, he wouldn't tell you, would he?' Rosie

said. 'I was coming back from the ladies' and another lecture from me mum about talking to strange men' – she nodded to Peter and James – 'and there he was, waiting for me, Whalemouth. He grabbed me by the arm and made a proposal that shook me for a minute. And when he wouldn't leave go of me I told him what I'd do with my foot.' She giggled now. 'I promised him that I would insert it straight up his' – and now she was actually laughing as she went on – 'nether regions until it came so far out of his big sloppy mouth that he'd be able to tie the laces. And when he still hung on to me, I kneed him in his delicate region, and I didn't slap his face but I punched it.'

By this time, her four listeners were bent double. Sally had heard the saying before about a boot being put up the nether regions, and in plain language, but it had never been expressed quite as forcibly as it had by Rosie.

Then bobbing on her seat, Rosie pointed out of the window. 'Not again! Here comes the starchy brigade.'

They all looked to see *Dogfish One* passing up the creek towards the berth at the top.

And now she explained to their enquiring faces: 'If we happen to berth where she is, her crew's up and off like a shot. But if she berths near us, without having first seen us, then the wind is in her tail and she's off again. One day I tried to get pally with the lady by patting her little dog. She told me its name, in a very polite voice. But she looked at me as if I was something the cat had brought in. Then she picks up the poor little thing, hugs it to her, and marches off. Our Phil, that's me young brother, says they always blow their noses loudly after passing us. It's to get rid of the smell of us.'

Peter said, 'Oh, my! Do you think they're as bad as that? They have their good side, you know, as Fred, our friend here, will tell you. He had a bit of a do with them before he left the bay – it was to do with a Latin quotation. So on the way to Yarmouth when he had his experience with a roller canvas cover, then found he couldn't move, Mrs C, here, had to take the dog out, which made them guess that something was wrong. They couldn't very well approach her; but they had heard through our loud-mouthed friend that we were berthed next to them. He was addressing me as Doctor, and so they came to me to see if I would look in on *Dogfish Three* to see if anything was wrong. This I did.'

Peter was now nodding towards Fred, who

said, 'And I'll always be grateful you did, Peter. Otherwise, I know I would have ended up in hospital.'

'And,' cried James now, 'the truth is you were terrified to leave your wife to two philandering sailor fellows.'

'You're quite right,' answered Fred, somewhat sheepishly, 'absolutely right.'

'Oh, Lord!' exclaimed Peter. 'Look at the time. We must be off. And it's such a pity. Look, Rosie. Keep in touch, will you? Send us a card, and tell us what's happening to you.' From his wallet he withdrew two printed cards. The top one he handed to Rosie, saying, 'That's my father's address, because if I were to get a card signed "Rosie" my wife would not believe it was from a fifteen-year-old, short-haired little vixen.'

'I'm not just fifteen; I'll be sixteen shortly.'

'Well, that would make it worse, a sixteen-year-old little vixen, and the nicest one James and I have ever met.'

'I second that, and third it,' put in James. 'And send me a card, too, Rosie. But not to the theological college, send it to my father. There's a fellow who would love to meet you. I haven't a card on me, but can you remember

The Reverend Philip Watson, The Vicarage, Burdet Road, London – East. Everybody knows the Rev. P – or Sandy as his friends know him. Can you remember that?'

'Yes, of course. That's one thing I do have, a marvellous memory for dates and things,' said Rosie.

There was a shaking of hands; then when both men stooped and kissed Rosie on the cheek, her face could have matched the colour of her cousin's red coiffure.

Within a few minutes Sally and Fred were standing in the stern waving goodbye to their new friends. The last words were from James, calling, 'Until we meet again!'

Rosie was now standing on the bank; she bent forward to pat Bill's head where he was standing, his front paws on the gunwale, and she said quietly, 'They're two lovely fellows, aren't they? And to think one's a doctor, and the other a parson. I'll never forget them.'

She straightened up as two men approached them from the big boat. The older one said to Rosie, 'We're just going looking to see if there's anywhere near we can have a drink, lass. We won't be long,' and Rosie said, 'Dad, these are Mr and Mrs Carpenter.'

The man leaned towards Sally and said, 'I'm very pleased to meet you, Mrs Carpenter,' and stretching his hand to Fred, he said, 'And you, sir, very pleased indeed. I hope you're staying for a time.'

'I wish we were,' said Fred, 'but we have to be off about four o'clock: we must cross Breydon, for our time is up on Saturday morning.'

'Oh, that's a pity,' the man said. 'But likely you'll be able to keep in touch with my lass.' He jerked his head towards Rosie. 'She'd like that.'

It was Sally who answered quickly, 'Oh, we mean to, we mean to. It's all been arranged.'

She noticed that the man looked slightly surprised, but very pleased, and his smile widened. He turned and, patting his daughter on the shoulder, said, 'Don't worry. Everything is going to be all right, you'll see.'

Sally had noticed that the other man, who was younger, had not waited; it was as though he was making it clear to them he had nothing to do with whatever was happening.

'May I pop back and see you before you leave?' said Rosie quietly.

'We should be very sorry if you didn't,' said Fred.

'OK, then, I'll be back.' And with this she

walked smartly away to the other boat . . .

Fred said, 'Her father seems a decent sort; it's a pity the same can't be said about her mother.'

Sally made lunch, and during it they talked about Rosie and her two new friends. Suddenly, just as Sally was saying, 'I think I should walk along to *Dogfish One* and thank them for their thoughtfulness that saved you a hospital trip,' there was the sound of raised voices from the far end of the bank. She got up, went out into the cockpit, leaned over the side, and there, along the bank, was the man from *Dogfish One* and the younger man from the big boat they had seen earlier, who was yelling, 'Aye, I can read and there's more bloody rubbish on this river than those few tins I've tossed there, and I'm lookin' at it now. And who the hell d'you think you are anyway with your tuppence-halfpenny little craft? And don't come your high and mighty tone with me, mister, else I'll soon put you in your place, and that'll be on your back. And another thing when I'm on. You tell that weak-kneed son of yours to keep his disdainful look off my womenfolk or else he'll be needing a set of false front teeth before he reaches port.'

There was silence as if his opponent was now

getting his oar in. Then the man's voice came again and now, on a mock laugh, 'Report, hell! Do that, mister. Do that; then I'll get a laugh, for you'll find out who you're reportin'.'

On this he returned to his boat and Sally could make out nothing further from the clamour of voices that greeted him.

She went back into the cabin and repeated to Fred all she had heard, ending, 'That's put the finishing touches to my visit. I wouldn't dare go along there now and visit them.'

Fred laughed. 'Well,' he said, 'there'll be plenty of time tomorrow morning before we leave Oulton; and I can do the talking then.'

Strangely, though, no sound whatever came from their neighbours during the next few hours; and finally Sally said, 'Look at the clock. I'm going to get something to eat. If Rosie doesn't come by soon, then we'll have to go.'

But as if Rosie herself had heard her speaking, there was a tap on the cabin door.

'Come on in, dear. We were just talking about you,' Sally called.

When Rosie reached the bottom of the steps she did not speak, and they looked at her in amazement.

Her face looked bloated; there was a bump on

her forehead, and her eyes were streaming with tears.

'Oh, my dear!' cried Sally. 'What is it? Sit down. Sit down. What's happened to your head and your face? Fred,' she turned to him, 'pour out some tea . . . And put a drop of brandy in it.'

Lying back against the bulkhead, Rosie muttered, 'It's all right. It's all right. My dad's sent me to tell you, anyway.'

Sally handed her the cup of tea, and she gulped at it; then drained the cup dry; after which she sighed; then looking from the one to the other of her hosts, she said, 'It was like this. After she got Dad out of the way she hauled me into my cabin, which is like a cubby-hole up in the bows, and, locking the door, she said, "Now you can cool your heels. That'll teach you to go visiting."

'I sat in my bunk, and I didn't mind because I had a book to read. I often buy a book just for its cover. This one was on a second-hand stall in Yarmouth market. It had a lovely leather back. I suppose it's a daft way to pick books, but I like the feel of them. This one, I saw, must have been an old one for it had a narrow red ribbon intended as a book marker. I had no idea what

it was about, only that it was in English and had
been translated from a French writer.' She was
now addressing herself wholly to Fred. 'Well, I
sat there, with my feet on the bunk, and started
to read. At first, it was quite ordinary, all about
some family, until it pointed out that the woman
had been unhappily married for years; her
husband had treated her really very roughly.
Well, I skipped pages and got the gist of it.
She was walking the dog along this path where
they were on holiday, and she comes across
this young fellow. Of course, being French, he
would have to be a painter. I skipped some
more, until I came to the part where they are
very much in love and in bed together.

'It was here that my mouth fell open, my eyes
bulged, and my hair seemed to stand on end, for
the scene dotted all the Is and crossed the Ts of
things that I never imagined could happen. It
made the woman in the book feel "*ecstasy*",
which was printed in capitals and so stood out.
I thought, that's what it must be like for some
people, and, fancy, her fifteen years older than
him.

'It was at that moment when my eyes were
glued to the page that the door flew open . . .
and there was Ma; and the book had had such

an effect on me that, for a second, I didn't seem to take her in before it was grabbed from my hands and she said, "You and your trash!" and then started to read the page. Her mouth dropped open and she cried at me, "Ecstasy! You dirty little bugger, you! Filthy, you are. Filthy!" I was now on my feet, and I faced her, and I cried at her, "You've had four of us, and I bet we didn't come by ecstasy. You haven't got it in you. You're just a big bladder of lard with a loud gob." It was at this she attacked me. She took me by the shoulders and banged my head against the woodwork until I went dizzy. Then she was punching me in the face, when me dad and Phil dragged her out.

'I must have blotted out for a few seconds, because I next remember my dad holding me and stroking my face, saying, "Don't worry, lass. She'll never lay hands on you again. Today she's put the finishing touches to herself and all her crew. Now listen: Phil will stay with you. I'm going to speak to her. There'll be no yelling, but I'll bring her along to this end where you'll be able to hear every word." '

Up till now, Rosie had been gabbling her news; but she suddenly stopped and, putting a hand across her eyes, she whimpered, 'I'm sorry.

I'm sorry. You people don't want to hear all this.'

Sally's voice was calm as she said, 'We do. We do, Rosie. Now come on, get it off your chest: finish what more there is to say. Just take your time.'

'May I have a drink of water, Mrs C?'

After sipping at the water, she looked at Bill, who had sidled along the seat and laid his head on her knee. And when he looked up at her, she stroked his face, saying brokenly, 'I do believe he's sorry for me.'

The other two said nothing; they just sat and waited. Then, still stroking Bill's head, she started to talk again, but slowly: 'I heard me dad speaking now; he was saying, "This is the end, Flo; and I'm not going to do any shouting, I'm just telling you quietly what I'm going to do. I'm taking the boat in today and finishing the cruise . . . Now, now! Keep your mouth closed for a moment," he said, "you haven't heard half of it yet. When we get in, I'm taking Rosie with me and we're going into a hotel for the night; and tomorrow morning we are making straight for my mother's. So from this, Flo, you'll get it that I'm leaving you. I should have done it seven years ago when I left your bed for the last time.

' "Rosie, Lucy and the lad were little then; so I stuck it out. However, what I'm doing now is only a week premature, because I was going to tell you when we got back that we were finished; in fact, I made arrangements on the Friday at the factory. It was after Belle Pollock met me at the station and told me you had sacked her for daring to come to work, as you said, 'dressed up in finery'. In fact, she was going to a wedding party straight from work, and because she had to travel some way she had come to work in her best dress. Of course, she had her pinny on, but it wasn't big enough to cover her dress. Well, I took her back with me to the factory, and I got them all together, the whole sixty-five of them, machinists and managers, and I told them of changes that were to be made: that they could come to work in whatever clothes they liked, so long as they weren't outrageous; that they wouldn't again ever take orders from my wife, for she wouldn't be coming back to the factory. I might as well tell you that I had already told Jackson that if you put your nose in the door, he had my permission to remove you forcibly . . . You needn't grind your teeth, Flo, or get your hands ready for punching because, although so far I have never laid a hand on you, I can promise you this, I would take some pleasure in doing so now; and you wouldn't see out of those two mean eyes of yours for days."'

Again Rosie paused; and the tears were now running slowly down her face. 'Eeh! I couldn't believe my ears, because that was me dad talking in a way I never imagined he could. He was saying, "The house is in my name only. Now you may stay in it until you might want to marry again; but once you have a fancy man in, you, dear Flo, will have to find other quarters. Anyway, I might want to sell it up.

'"Now, I'll leave you an allowance, which'll be sufficient, but that's all, just sufficient to keep you, and the boy and young Lucy at school. One thing, you won't keep Phil for very long; he wants to come along with me even now; but I shall leave him in charge, sort of. But I assure you that the allowance you're going to get won't keep you and your family and nieces and nephews in food and funds. So you'll likely be seeing much less of them than you've been used to.

'"One final piece of information for you, Flo: I'm moving the factory down to the south within the next few months, in order to be near my mother."

'Now I heard Mum speak for the first time. It was a scream: "And your fancy woman!" and Dad answered her, quite quickly. "Yes, and to be near my fancy woman, Flo; but also in order to see that my Rosie gets an education."

' "God!" It was Mum screaming again. "Your Rosie educated? The only education she's fit for will be to turn her out as a whore."

'I couldn't believe what my dad said next: "Well, if she does, Flo, there's one thing sure. She'll make a better job at it than you ever did, or could."

'Now Mum did scream, and Dad shouted, "Now I warned you. Alec! You'd better come and get your aunt away. You've been all ears, so you'll have heard all about it. And likely you'll have to tie her down for the next few days." And with this, Dad came back to me. His chest was heaving as though he had been running, and Phil said to him, "Sit down, Dad. Sit down."

' "No, lad. No. There'll be no sitting down for me until I get off this boat, Rosie with me."

'He now pulled me to my feet, saying, "Go along, lass, and say goodbye to your friends. You can tell them all that's happened, and seeing, as you say, the fellow's a teacher and she is a nice woman, they'll understand. Anyway, don't come back on board until you see me. Then you must stick close by me during the rest of the time we're here. If she gets her hands on you, she'll murder you. I know that." '

She stopped talking now, and Fred and Sally just sat staring at her, as though they had nothing to say. Yet Sally had never felt so sorry for anyone in her life as she did for that young girl; and she knew Fred was feeling the same.

Spontaneously they leaped from their seats: Sally pushed Bill onto the floor, and they sat, one on each side of her, and held her hands, and Fred said, 'Don't worry, my dear. It's a wonderful thing your father's doing for you.'

What Sally did then was to put her arms around the girl and hug her. Her arms around Sally's neck, Rosie cried openly; then, pulling herself away, she dried her eyes and, looking at Fred, she said, 'About education, Mr Carpenter; it's going to be tough because somehow, what-ever school I go to I can't help being myself. You see, from what I read, I've got a lot of words in my head; and I know where I should use them; but when I get angry or really mad or someone slights me, it's swear words that come out.'

'Oh, Rosie, Rosie. My back's still bad; don't make me laugh, please. But if you want my advice about your education, let me say this to you. Before your father attempts to get you into some posh school, I would advise that you put yourself in the hands of a tutor for six months or so. He or she will prepare you for the kind of education I think you need and will file down the rough edges like your language. You understand what I mean?'

'Oh, yes, I do, Mr C. Yes, I do, because I know I would make a fool of myself if I went to one of those posh places straight away. The job will be getting Dad to see it.'

'Well, I can tell you, Rosie, that one day you will laugh and look back on this swearing period as a huge joke, because we're going to keep in touch, aren't we, Sally?'

'Of course. Of course. Look: I'll give you our phone number and address. And as soon as you get settled into your grandma's, give us a ring. We'll be home by Saturday night . . . Another thing, your father is moving your factory south; and we live not far from London, at Hastings. You must come for the weekend whenever you feel like it. Now, you will, won't you?'

'Oh, yes; yes. And it's wonderful of you to want me.'

'It'll be wonderful to have you,' said Fred.

'And your father,' his wife put in, 'and your granny; we have plenty of room to spare.'

A voice from above said quietly, 'Dad's waiting, Rosie,' at which she sprang up, saying, 'I'll be away, then. And you're getting off your-selves.' She flung her arms round Sally's neck again, saying now, 'Oh, I'm so glad I've met you; you've been so nice to me, better than anyone I've ever known.'

She put her hand out to Fred, adding, 'And I want to be educated, Mr Carpenter. I really do.'

'And you will, Rosie. Never you fear, you will.'

They followed her into the cockpit and watched her run along with her brother to where her father was waiting for her on the river bank.

4

It was early evening on Friday when Sally watched her husband mooring *Dogfish Three* by ropes through the rings in the stone wall that lay outside the boatyard. Luckily, she hadn't to get out to bring in the rond anchors, which chore she had been doing since the event on Breydon Water at the beginning of the holiday – Fred's back was still bad. Now, he had allowed about two foot of ropeway for mooring.

The first thing she said was not 'Thank God I'm almost on dry land,' although that's what she was thinking; but stooping to Bill, she said, 'Come on, dear; I know you're bursting; you've been such a good boy,' and, together, they jumped ashore, and he took her at a rush to the nearest scrub.

Ten minutes later, they returned to *Dogfish*

Three, now bobbing happily up and down just a foot from the wall. No more muddy banks or nervously traversing a wooden gangway to reach a path; no more dreaming of sinking or drowning; they were almost home.

They had arrived rather late for berthing, yet there were still more boats coming in, and they didn't know if Rosie's boat was one of them.

Fred, once again the Captain, had suddenly become very quiet. Sally said to him, 'You're tired, aren't you? We're past talking any more tonight about the wonderful people we've met during these last few days. Look, darling, you put your feet up and I'll make us something light, then get to bed. We'll continue our talking tomorrow, and the next day, and the next.'

With a sigh, her husband did as he was bidden, but catching her hand as she passed him and looking up at her, he said, 'You know something? You're the most wonderful woman in the world, for how you have managed this awful week, and me, I'll never know.'

She bent and kissed him on the nose, saying airily, 'Well, I'll remind you every day henceforth of those words.' With this, she put the kettle on; and that was all she could later recall doing until . . .

What time was it when she woke with the most odd feeling? Something was pressing against her, pushing her, and she wasn't lying properly. What was it? She opened her eyes and immediately thought there must be something wrong with her sight. There was the floor, not three inches from her nose. Fred seemed to be pushing her towards it. Not only that, the cups on the hooks above a cabinet at the end of the bunk bed were now hanging in the air. She went to lift herself up and away from Fred but rolled onto the floor and screamed. The noise brought Fred awake as she yelled, 'We've toppled over! We're sinking!'

Like two drunkards, they crawled sideways into the cockpit, where Sally screamed again, for *Dogfish Three* was, quite literally, hanging up on the wall, well out of the water.

Fred was now climbing the wall and groping at the grass. She could just make him out through the coming dawn.

When the stern of the boat fell with a crash into the water she screamed again, for now she had fallen into the saloon. When the second crash came she knew it was the end, for when the bows hit the water she was bounced once more into a sitting position, this time with Bill jumping all over her and adding his howls to hers.

'Shut up, woman! Shut up! We're all right. It's the tide. It's going down.'

'W-w-why didn't you think of that when you moored us to those rings, Mr Big-head? You had your bl-bl-blooming map to go by – swear by.'

By then they were back to normal. Sally's voice and Bill's barking were suddenly cut off by a series of yells and screams. The noise they were making had apparently alerted others to the situation and there was further plop-plopping of boats back into the water.

The bank was alive with people. Apparently Captain Carpenter wasn't the only one who hadn't taken into account the falling tide – and the wall.

He was now in his trousers and he pulled Sally to her feet saying, 'It's all right. It's all right now. Look, I'll get you a cup of tea. And put your dressing-gown on, you're shivering.' It struck her that it was she who should have been saying, 'Careful, dear. Mind your back.' Instead, she was letting him get the tea – she needed it.

'A dramatic finish to the week. What d'you say?' said the Captain casually.

'A finish that I could have done without,' his wife replied.

He did not remark on this but said, 'Cup of hot tea, eh? I'll put the kettle on.'

It was as he did so that they heard a high cry, almost a scream, and were once again on their feet in the stern well, where they ascertained that the cries weren't coming from the bank but from somewhere along the line of boats.

Leaning over the bows, Fred saw immediately the reason for the commotion. 'It's a little dog in the river swimming down this way, at least trying to.'

Sally looked along the bank and saw the woman from *Dogfish One*. She was looking in between each boat, yelling as she did so, 'She can't swim! She can't swim! She'll drown! She'll drown!'

Sally leaned over the bows and saw the small animal struggling to swim.

Fred grabbed a boat-hook from the top of the cabin, then hung far out over the side of the boat, saying to Sally, 'Hang on to me!'

She grabbed him around the hips, crying, 'Mind your back! And I can't hold you, you'll fall!'

When, at last, at the third attempt, Fred

managed to manoeuvre the end of the boat-hook into the dog's collar, a kind of muffled cheer went up from the line of boats, and slowly he drew the little animal towards him. But as he leaned further still over the side to lift the drenched, frightened body from the water he naturally let go of the boat-hook, which slid silently from his hand and into the fast-flowing stream. Now came the task of pulling him and the animal up together.

What moment of bravery urged Sally to bend almost as far over as he had and take the sodden little beast from his grip she never knew. She was aware only that there were other people in the stern well. One was a woman, and she had her arms about her, pulling her back on to *terra firma* while two male figures hoisted Fred aboard. And there they all were. Sally found herself sitting clutching the shivering animal to her, with its owner staring down at her, and Fred was half lying on the forecastle seat gasping as their friend from *Dogfish One* and his son bent towards him alternately talking at him. Sally heard Fred say now, 'I'm all right, I'm all right. Only don't touch my back.'

The woman was speaking to Sally now as she held out her hands for her pet, who seemed reluctant to leave her rescuer. She was saying, 'She's terrified of water. She can't swim; we've tried to get her to but she can't. I don't know how she got that far. I can't thank your husband enough. I don't know how it happened, I just don't. Perhaps she jumped because she was afraid of the boat capsizing again.'

Sally smiled to herself. So they were another pair of idiots who hadn't read the time of the tide going down.

'She's old, you see, but we love her.' The woman hugged the animal to her as if she were a child, and likely she was to her as Bill was to Fred and herself, Sally realised. She heard herself say shakily, 'We are dog people too. We love Bill although everyone thinks he's ugly.'

'Oh, he's not. He's not. Look how my Sue took to him.' She laughed. 'She was quite brazen, wasn't she?' Definitely she was their friend indeed now. They were all their friends. How funny. How really funny. Sally had to suppress the desire to laugh. But then the realisation came at her: if Fred had slipped right over he could swim, he was a good swimmer, yet with that back and the tide running down fast, if he had then caught hold of the dog, what might have happened? You never knew.

She heard herself say quietly, 'I should take her home and give her a warm bath and some hot milk.'

'Yes, yes.' The woman was smiling and nodding. 'Yes, I'll do that right away.' She turned to her husband, saying, 'I must get her back and give her a warm bath.'

'Yes. Yes, my dear.' But it was the son who helped her out onto the bank, while the man turned to Sally, and they looked at each other eye to eye for a moment before he said quietly, 'Sorry for all the fazzle there has been. Pity we didn't get to know you sooner. Our fault. Oh, yes, our fault. Thanks. Thanks all the same.'

'It's I who should be thanking you, for suggesting to Dr Wheeler that he should look in on my husband. Otherwise, Fred would have been in hospital.'

The man answered with a nod, saying, 'Oh, that was nothing. Nothing.' Then he turned to Fred and said, 'We'll have a word later, but I must see to my wife now. Thank you. Thank you.'

As he jumped ashore, the boy, who had come back, now stepped into the boat and, looking at Fred, he said, 'Thank you, sir. My mother would have gone crazy if she had lost Sue. And about the other evening, sir: I'm sorry for my manner towards you.' And then he admitted, quite humbly, 'We are new to the river and, like all newcomers, we imagine we know it all, but we'll learn.'

'Get along now, son, and see to your mother.'

'Thanks, sir. Thank you, Mrs Carpenter.' He nodded towards Sally then stepped out onto the bank again.

After a moment, Sally looked at Fred and said, 'Your back's paining, isn't it? Come on!' She took his arm and they went down into the cabin, where she said to him, 'Sit yourself down. There's no need to rush; we'll get home today, some time.'

'You're right. You know, I love boats, and I've loved the river, you know I have, but I've never longed to be at home so much as I do at this minute.'

PART TWO

Afterwards

5

The carpenters arrived home that Saturday night after an awful journey of taxis, porters, trains – taxis, porters, trains – taxis, porters, trains. In the last train, because of Bill, as on their journey out, they spent it in the guard's van.

As usual, the house was like an ice-box. It consisted of eight large rooms with no central heating in any of them. It had belonged to an old aunt of Sally's mother, and Sally herself had lived in it for twenty-one years, bar the war evacuation, and Fred for eighteen of those years, and the only heating they had ever had in the kitchen was a small covered-in coke stove that gave them hot water – the old kitchen range had been taken out. At one time most of the cooking must have been done in the scullery, but the range there also had been removed.

Under the window was a shallow sink, with a draining-board attached. All the cooking was now done on an electric stove.

A friend of Sally's, once, seeing this set-up, said to her, 'And you don't have any help? Well, all I can say is that the Archangel Gabriel, the organiser up there, must send down a gang of off-duty angels to give you a hand because nobody else could turn out the meals you do on that thing.' And sometimes Sally thought that some help, heavenly or earthly, would have been very welcome.

Now, on their return, Bill was delighted to be back, in spite of the cold, and she and Fred had dumped all their gear in the hall. Within half an hour they had made a pot of coffee and some bacon sandwiches, and now the three of them were sitting as close to the little electric fire in the study as they could get, with Bill's nose almost on the bars.

After two cups of coffee and his sandwiches, Fred sighed and said, 'Just leave these things as they are. We're going to bed.'

'What if Rosie should phone? She said she would.'

'Well let her phone; you're not coming down those stairs tonight.'

'How's your back?' Sally asked.

'Well,' he replied, 'let's say I know I've got one, and I suppose I shall have pain for some little time.'

Fifteen minutes later Bill was tucked up in his basket in the corner of the bedroom and his owners were lying under three woollen blankets.

'Good night, Captain.'

'Good night, First Mate,' Fred answered, and they both laughed.

That was all Sally remembered until the following morning when she awoke to Fred standing by her side, saying, 'Would you like this?'

'Good gracious! What time is it?'

'Twenty-five minutes to ten.'

'What! Have you been up long?'

'About twenty minutes,' he said.

'How're you feeling?' she asked.

'Well, dear,' he said, 'all I can say at the moment is, I'm glad to be back. How're you feeling?'

'Tired. May I stay in bed all day?'

'No; you may not, woman; there's work waiting for us both downstairs. Now drink that tea while it's hot . . .'

The day passed quickly. They cleared the gear in the hall, and brought in enough logs for Fred to get a good wood fire going in the drawing room. It was one of the two rooms that had a large fireplace, the other was the hall; but that was only ever lit at Christmas time or if they had visitors.

Fred spent the day mostly in the drawing room preparing his school work. Sally had her time filled with creating a makeshift lunch out of the tins they had brought home with them, and preparing the washing for the following day – they did not have a washing-machine or drier.

It was now just turned six o'clock. They had finished tea and Fred was sitting beside her on the sofa opposite the blazing logs. Bill was curled in front of the broad hearth; everything was peaceful; they were back to normal and were now waiting for Rosie's phone call.

It never came. It wasn't until Wednesday evening, just after their meal, that they heard from Rosie of the River, as Sally liked to think of her.

'Is that you, Mrs C?'

'Yes, Rosie; it's me. How are you?'

'Oh, Mrs C . . . Oh, Mrs C, you won't believe it. This is Paradise. I can't believe I'm going to live here for good; and me granny's lovely. Sharp-tongued, you know, like me, but she's lovely. And there are three servants – well, I mean there's a cook and a maid and a lady, 'cos she is a lady. They call her Miss Collins and she looks after Grandma – that is, when she needs her; other times she sees to the housekeeping. I would say she's like a glorified housekeeper. And she's been so nice to me. Me dad's so happy, too. I've never seen him like this before. What d'you think he's gone and done, Mrs C? Go on, have a guess.'

'I couldn't guess, Rosie. I haven't an idea in my head what you or your dad will do next.'

'Well, I'll tell you. He made an appointment with the head of a ladies' school. Aye, he did; and he came back full of it; and me granny said, "Oh, my! You would aim high, wouldn't you? That's a very posh place." I don't mind telling you, Mrs C, that made me have the jitters, because I know how some of those bitches would look upon the likes of me, especially if I came out with a mouthful . . . Is Mr C there?'

'Yes; I'm here, Rosie.' Fred was now at his wife's elbow. 'How are things?'

'Well, Mr C, I'll tell you how they are. And they're all through you and what you said to me.

It made me think. You know, Dad cannot see me as other people do. To him I'm a bright spark, and he would expect that headmistress to see me as such. So, you know what you said? I should be coached and be prepared for a good school by having a sort of private tutor. You remember?'

'Yes; yes, I do.'

'Well, it was no good putting that from me, but I thought he might take it from . . . well, somebody . . . I'll tell you what I did. I made up me mind to go and have a word with that headmistress before Dad got at her and let her actually see what she would be taking on.'

'You didn't!'

'I did, Mr C. It was like this. I did what you said and I found my own way to the school, and the first person I spoke to was a tall reedy miss, who, after looking me up and down, decided I had come to the wrong place; and what did I want?

'"I want to speak to the Headmistress," I said.

'"I am sorry, the Headmistress is busy," she said.

'"She'll see me," I said.

'"The Headmistress is busy," she snapped

back at me, and in very distinct English, Mr C.'

Fred laughed; and Rosie went on, ' "Busy or not busy," I said, "you tell her that Rosie Stevenson wants to see her, whose father has an appointment with her this afternoon about me coming to this school . . ."

'I didn't get any further, Mr C. You wouldn't believe it. She looked at me amazed and said, "What?"

'I said, "Yes, what! You heard what I said, miss. Tell her that I am Rosie Stevenson who is coming with my father this afternoon about . . ." You know what she said next? "I think you have come to the wrong school."

' "No, Miss," I said; "I haven't come to the wrong school." And you know what I did then, Mrs C? I thought about you and how you stand and how you speak, so I pushed my head up, pulled my chin in, thrust my shoulders back and in as near your voice as I could attempt I said, "Will you kindly go to your headmistress and give her my message, and bring the result back to me here, *please*!" I stressed the please. She now stared at me as if I were something from another planet. But she did what I said. And you know? You wouldn't believe it. If she had been kicked in the' – she was chuckling now – 'the nether regions she couldn't have been back quicker; but I've no words to describe the look she gave me. Anyway, the next minute it seemed I was sitting in a seat opposite the Headmistress, and after we'd exchanged long weighing-up glances, she said, "You wish to see me about the appointment you and your father have with me this afternoon?"

'"Just that, Miss," I said.

'"Well, go on," she said, "I'm waiting."

'"Well, it's like this, Miss. I'll put me cards on the table. I know I'm not fit yet to come to your school and a schoolmaster friend of mine put it plainly to me what I should do."

'"You have a schoolmaster friend?" she said.

'"Aye, I have," I said; "and he teaches maths in a grammar school."

'"Oh. And which grammar school is that?"

'"In Hastings, ma'am. And he's been to Oxford."

'She smiled, and I think she almost laughed. I didn't know whether you'd been to Oxford or Cambridge but I knew you must have been to some big university, so I picked on Oxford.'

Fred was laughing again as he said, 'You did right there, Rosie, you did right there. Go on. Go on.'

'Well, she said to me, "And what idea has this schoolmaster put into your head about your education?"

'"Well, Miss," I said, "he advised me to have at least six months' tuition in English and learning how to . . ." Well, you see, it's like this. I got all flummoxed here, Mrs C, and I had to be meself, so I just blurted out, "I've got the habit of swearing. I read a lot, oh, I read piles and I've got all the words in me head and I know where they should go, but when people get nasty or look down their nose at me I get ratty, and so I use my own language at them."

'"And your own language is what?" she said.

'"Well, you could say bad language, ma'am," I said.

'"You use bad language?" she said.

"Oh," I put in here, "I don't mean four-letter words – I never use those – it's just bloody, bugger, damn and blast, and things like that, and they come out instead of the words I want to use."'

She started to giggle again, saying, 'D'you know what happened next?'

Laughing her head off, Sally suggested, 'She fell across the table in a dead faint.'

'No, she didn't. She was on one of those swing

chairs and she swung round to the bookcase that was close behind her and she started sorting some books out, picking them up one after the other; and then finally she brought out a thin one and turned back and put it on the table, and I knew quite well she hadn't been looking for a book. You know people do funny things when they're trying to stop themselves laughing? Her face was straight now but her eyes were bright. Then she said, "And your schoolmaster friend advised you to put your cards on the table, as you said, and take six months' tuition before coming to this school?"

'"Yes," I answered. "He told me that I shouldn't say anything to my dad about it but should come to you and you would put it across to him as if it was your idea, 'cos he'd listen to you where he wouldn't listen to me, about spending six months in learning not to swear and to talk properly, because he would say that's what he was sending me to this school for."

'And now, listen, Mr C, to what she said next. It was just this. "You know, I think your school-master friend is a very clever and far-seeing gentleman. His suggestion was right and I think I know the very person who could take control of your situation." And she now rang a bell, and when the lady with the stupefied face appeared, she said, "Miss Nesbit, please ask Jean to prepare coffee for two, and take Rosie into my sitting room." Then, looking at me and lifting her hand, she indicated I should follow the now gaping Miss Nesbit. Well, not only did I follow her, I walked beside her down this long corridor, and I looked at her and her mouth was wide open and, you know, being me still . . . well, don't laugh, I'd laid my cards on the table, hadn't I? – I wasn't yet educated, I was still me, Rosie, so I looked at her' – she began to laugh – 'it was awful of me I suppose, but I couldn't help it. "Well," I said, "I should close my mouth if I were you, there's lots of flies still about, wasps especially. They hibernate at this time of the year, you know."

'She stopped dead in her tracks and her mouth seemed to get wider before she snapped it closed, and then she said, "You are an insulting creature."

'"Well," I answered her, "I'm bound to be, aren't I? 'Cos, you know, I'm from another planet. You've never seen anything like me in this school before, have you?" And she answered, "No, I haven't; and I trust that I never shall."

151

'And now I did follow her, because she strolled away towards a door, opened it wide, stepped aside, and when I'd passed her she banged it closed behind me, almost taking my heels off me. But that voice inside me, you know, which tells me off, said, "You go too far at times."'

There was a short silence now on the line, during which Fred and Sally exchanged glances that were partly sad. Then Rosie broke in again, 'I was all wobbly inside, really frightened somehow. My brave face had slipped and I thought, what if she goes to the Headmistress and tells her I insulted her. Well, it was done. I had done it again. I hoped I hadn't made a mess of things. Oh, yes, I was saying to myself, "You can be too clever, Rosie Stevenson," when the Headmistress came in – by the way, her name is Miss Clarke – and I had the sense to stand up. She said, "Sit down. Sit down." Her voice was very nice, quite friendly, so I couldn't tell if the woman had spoken about me or not. "How do you like your coffee, black or white?" she said.

'For a minute I was stumped, and then I stammered, "I've never had much choice, I take it as it comes; but I think I would like it white."

'"I do too," she said. "Nowadays, people

152

take it black with just a knob of cream on the top, but I think that's just a fashion for the restaurants. Now" – she had poured out the coffee and handed me a cup, and it rattled in the saucer, I can tell you, when I took it. She didn't let on, but said, "I have spoken to Miss Barrington. She's the lady I have in mind who might be able to help you. She used to work here. Well, she worked here for twenty years up till two years ago, when her health gave out. She takes on a pupil now and again in order to keep her hand in, because she's a fine linguist. If she wishes to take on another pupil, I shall put it over to your father, as you did with me today. Well" – and now, Mr C, she laughed – "at least I should say, I shall put your friendly schoolmaster's idea over to him, but as if I had thought the whole matter up myself." Wasn't that nice of her?'

Fred said, 'Indeed it was. She must be a very nice lady altogether.'

'You know what she asked me next? Well it was, had I any idea what I wanted to be, and all I could say was' – now she gave a little laugh as she added – 'and I said it in one word, and that was "educated". And she laughed at this and said, "Well, when you're educated, have you any idea what you'd like to be?" and I said, "No, ma'am, except I think I'll know then, when I can speak English properly and perhaps a language. I'll know then what I'll want to be." '

There was a pause on the line and a noise coming from somewhere as Rosie yelled, 'All right! All right! I'm coming,' and then in a lower voice, 'It's Dad. He's just come in; I'll have to go. I'll tell you the rest tomorrow. If not, the day after. It's funny, but all I want to do is to talk to you both and tell you what's happening to me, 'cos you know you were the cause of it. Yes, you were. Bye-bye.'

'There's one thing I'm glad about,' Sally said to her husband as they turned from the phone. 'She's already recognised the still small voice.'

'You're right there, dear. I wonder what this Miss Barrington will be like. She'll have to be a woman of deep understanding and patience to alter our Rosie.'

They didn't hear anything further from Rosie for two days, and it was Saturday again, just one week from the day they had arrived home so weary, so tired, so cold after their holiday on the river. But Saturday didn't go without its surprises. Fred had just come in from school at half past twelve – the grammar school worked on a Saturday morning – and he had just finished saying, 'Any news in the post?' and Sally had answered, 'No,' when there came a ring at the bell. When she opened the door there was a van outside on which was printed in large letters 'J. W. Fawcett, Hosier', and underneath 'Let us sock it to you'. The man on the steps was holding out a large parcel to her and smiling as he said, 'Special delivery, ma'am. With the compliments of J. W. Fawcett.'

'Thank you,' she said. 'Thank you,' taking the large box into her arms. 'Is there anything to pay?'

'No, nothing whatever. Nothing whatever.' And on this, still smiling, he turned about and walked back to his van and drove off. She turned to Fred, who had come into the hall, and said, 'Not only special delivery but pleasantly delivered. Did you ever see such a bright face?'

'What is it?'

'How do I know? He says it's special delivery, and there it is: it has our name and address on correctly. Look what's written on the side.'

He now took it from her and held it at arm's length, and she began to laugh as she read the beautifully scrolled words in black and gold written along one side of the parcel, SOCK IT TO THEM IN EVERY CORNER OF THE WORLD, and said, 'It's got something like that written on the van.' They looked at each other and Fred, laughing now, said, 'Sock it to them in every corner of the world. Who on earth is this from?'

As he was attempting to tear the coloured ribbon from the box, his wife said, 'Look, don't tear it, please! Let's cut it: we must keep that cover, whoever it's from. Get the scissors.'

He was back in the dining room within seconds. As they cut away the paper a large cardboard box was revealed, out of which they took several packages. The first they opened was addressed to Sally, and as she held them up she couldn't believe her eyes: it was six pairs of silk stockings, real silk stockings. The next one was the biggest parcel and it was addressed to Fred. He spent no time in opening it to reveal a pair of football socks with his actual school colours knitted around the top in two bands, also a pair of brown woollen gloves. They too had the school colours ringing the wristbands. Then there was a round box, like a miniature hat box, and in it was a woollen pull-on hat like those that skiers often wear. The last parcel was quite bulky. It was addressed to 'Mr Bill' and, on opening it, there was a most lovely dog's coat, green wool with brown leather strappings underneath and a card which said, 'With love from Sue to Bill'.

'The Mancunians!'

And now Fred repeated, 'Yes, the Mancunians. Would you ever believe it? He must have a hosiery business. But how kind, and how—'

He stopped for words and Sally put in, 'Yes, how different from how we saw them and how we felt about them. This is because you saved the dog.'

'Yes, and on top of this we mustn't forget their thoughtfulness in getting me a doctor, otherwise I might still be in hospital. I know that, because my back was in a dreadful state.'

'Well I never!'

Again simultaneously they sat down on two of the dining-room chairs, and Fred said, 'And his sense of humour, "Sock it to them in every corner of the world". What an advert. You can't imagine him thinking up anything like that, can you?'

'I'll have to phone him straight away,' Sally said. 'It's going to be embarrassing, all of these things and such quality. Anyway,' she rose again, saying quickly now, 'let's take them into the drawing room; it's warmer there, and we can discuss what I have to say . . . and, of course, what you have to say.'

'Oh, no! No! No discussion about what we're going to say, that's the wrong thing: just say what's in our hearts and minds at that moment. I thought you'd be the one to say that.'

'Yes, you always expect me to say things for you, but I'm not going to do that this time. I'll say what I think, then I'll hand the phone over to you. You're the hero in this business anyway.'

'Hero be damned!'

They gathered up the things from the table, went into the drawing room and placed them at the end of the couch; and when Sally went to sit down he said, 'No, don't sit down; go and do it now.'

'All right, I'll do it now if you'll come with me because, don't forget, in all this business you were the smarty, coming out with your Latin quips as we sailed out into the blue.'

Sally dialled the number that was stamped on the end of the box, and they looked at each other as they waited while the bell rang at the other end of the line.

When a voice said, 'Yes; this is Fawcett here,'

she turned her head quickly and looked into the mouth of the phone as if she were seeing him, and said, 'What am I going to say to you, Mr Fawcett?'

'Oh. Hello! It arrived, then? Mrs Carpenter, is it?'

'Yes, it's Mrs Carpenter here, Mr Fawcett. And what a surprise! And how we have laughed: who on earth thought up that wonderful slogan?'

'Not me, I can tell you.'

Sally knew by his tone that he was laughing, but she couldn't imagine the man they knew laughing: her mental picture showed him still very straight-faced and he was saying, 'It was my son, when he was about seven years old. He came in from school one day full of himself: they had been playing football and his side had won, and he exclaimed loudly, "We socked it to 'em, Daddy, and as the master said, we sent them all home in parcels to their mummies." I had to laugh because we're an old-established firm and we had never gone in for any blatant advertising, but that term just struck me: didn't we make socks, among other things, and didn't we parcel them up and send them to our clients in different parts of the country? And so I put it to my father: we were in an age of competition and we should go with the times. He wasn't for it then, but I put a notice in the shop window, saying, "Why not let us sock it to your friends or family in any part of the country? Fawcett range from babies' bootees to anything you fancy in wool, silk or synthetics."'

There was a pause, and Fred put in, 'What happened next, Mr Fawcett? Did your father get angry?'

'No. No, Mr Carpenter; he just stood back and waited, and believe it or not, those words doubled our trade within a year. They seemed to attract a younger kind of client. We now have eight vans, each with its cheery driver. My wife considers it vulgar. But trade is trade.'

'I think it's marvellous,' Sally said. 'And that parcel, well, we thought, was unique. But you . . . you are so kind. We have done nothing to deserve all these beautiful things.'

'You saved Sue. If that dog had drowned, Mrs Carpenter, my wife would've been devastated. She simply adores that animal. We all love Sue; but to my wife she is something special, because she was given to her by her father the day before he died in a riding accident. That's just on ten years ago.'

'Oh, I'm so sorry. We are both sorry,' said Fred.

'There's one thing I can assure you of, Mr Carpenter, that she will always be in your debt. There's hardly a day passes but she mentions how brave you were, because we heard later that your back was still in a very poor condition and if you had slipped over the side you would never have been able to make it in that swift-flowing river. I shudder now when I think about it. How is your back?'

'Much better, thanks. And now it's my turn to say thank you because if you hadn't been kind enough to go to Peter, I mean Dr Wheeler, I should at this moment, I am sure, still be in hospital.'

'Oh, what I did was nothing, nothing.'

'What you did, Mr Fawcett,' Sally put in, 'wasn't nothing: it was a great kindness, and I'm so sorry we got off to such a bad start; and I must apologise for my husband's bad manners and his big head in quoting Horace's Odes.'

At this point Fred said, 'And I got my answer, didn't I? You see, it was our first trip on the river.'

'Oh,' replied Mr Fawcett, 'you weren't alone in that; it was our first too. But I'm afraid it's going to be our last. You see, I . . . well, my son and I like the water and we were for buying a boat, but my wife wasn't. However, we begged her just to try a week on the Broads. We had heard such good reports of the place. But they never mention Breydon Water, do they?'

'No,' Sally put in, on a laugh, 'they don't. And how I hate that stretch. In fact, I don't like rivers at all, it's my husband here who's mad on them.'

'Oh,' said Mr Fawcett now, 'my wife will be so pleased to hear that because it has decided us that it'll be no use us getting a boat because she will never come on it. I've never seen her so happy and pleased for years as she was when we returned home on that Saturday night. She'll be so glad to learn she's not the only one in the world who hates rivers. However, I've promised to get a better car and a nice travelling caravan. Yet it's amazing how she doesn't seem to mind when she's on a liner. I think it's because she can sit down in the saloon and not see that there's water outside the window. By the way, you're not all that distance from London, are you?'

'About a two-hour journey.'

'Well, we come up at least once a year to see a play or something like that. Wouldn't it be fine if we could all meet up one weekend? I know she would love that, and so would Walter. Oh, yes, he would love that.'

'That's a good idea,' Fred said, glancing at his wife. 'Perhaps it could be arranged towards Christmas some time; there are some very good shows on then.'

'Yes. Yes. We must talk again,' said Mr Fawcett. 'By the way, my name is James; my wife is Jessie and my boy is called Walter.'

Sally laughed here, and said, 'Well, we're Sally and Fred and, of course, Bill.'

Mr Fawcett laughed. 'Oh, no! we mustn't forget Bill. Jessie couldn't get over the fact that Sue fell in love with him.'

'Nor could we, because, you see, he hates dogs. When he was a puppy he was badly mauled by a labrador; but he loves people, adores people. And then he goes and falls for your Sue.'

'She isn't very friendly, and that she should have fallen for Bill . . . well, we couldn't get over it.

'Anyway, we must talk again. I'm so glad the parcel arrived, but more so that I have been able to talk to you both. It makes me feel that that holiday was not in vain because we ourselves seemed to see far too much of that awful family on the holiday cruiser. Dear, dear! What people! Anyway, goodbye for now; and I hope we'll all be meeting shortly.'

'Goodbye,' Fred said. 'Goodbye. And thank you again for those lovely presents.'

The phone was put down and the Carpenters looked at each other. Sally said quietly, ' "*That awful family*". Our poor Rosie! What would they think of her? Dear, dear, dear. What a mixture!'

They went back into the drawing room, sat down and looked at all the goodies that had been in the box, and Fred said, 'I can understand quite well how he felt about that lot. Except for Rosie and her father, I would have felt the same. What about you?'

Sally did not answer at first, but thought, Yes, it was pure snobbery thinking about them the way we did, but they *were* a dreadful lot, and so she said, 'Yes. Yes, I would have thought as he did, except for Rosie. But if either of them had heard Rosie at her best . . .' She raised her eyes heavenwards. 'Dear Lord, the reaction! If they ever do meet her, let's hope by that time the tutor has rid her of the bloody buggers, and so on.'

*　　*　　*

Later that evening, when they were both working in the study, Fred at his textbooks, Sally on her stock sheets, the phone rang once again. She said, 'If I didn't think that was Rosie, I wouldn't get up to answer it, because it's never stopped going all day.'

When she got to the phone a voice said, 'Hello there!' and she replied, 'Is that you, Rosie?'

Fred, who had flown from the study, shouted into the mouthpiece, 'Who else does she think it is?'

'This, Mr Frederick Carpenter,' came the reply, 'I would inform you, is Miss Rosina Stevenson, calling to enquire after Mr Bill Carpenter.'

'Whatever's the matter with you?' cried Sally. 'What's all this about?' and it was Rosie's normal voice that now came at her, saying, 'You'd never believe it if you saw me. Guess how I'm dressed. Go on! Have a guess.'

Fred answered quickly, 'In see-through tights.'

'Oh, Mr C! Mr C! How could you suggest such a thing. But I'll get into them any time you like.'

'Shut up, you two! Don't be silly. How *are* you dressed?' Sally asked now.

'Well, listen. Imagine me in a warm brown-coloured two-piece corded suit, skirt, pink silk shirt blouse, and below, wearing cavalry-coloured stockings with shoes to match, inch heels and slip-ons into the bargain. But that's not all, a brown suede bag with matching gloves. So what d'you think of that?'

'No wonder the mirror cracked when you looked into it,' put in Fred.

'Be quiet, Fred,' Sally said reproachfully. 'You've been shopping, Rosie? Who took you?'

'Miss Barrington; and from now on you're going to hear a lot about Miss Barrington, let me tell you.'

'Well, get on with it. What happened at the meeting?'

'Oh, that! Well, I'll try to cut it short. You know we had to meet Miss Clarke on the Monday afternoon and she told Dad of her, I repeat her, great idea of having me tutored in order that I should come up to the level of those young ladies who wished to enter her school. She didn't exactly put it like that but she made it plain to him, and he said, "Tutored for six months!" and to this she answered, "Yes, Mr Stevenson, and perhaps longer. It all depends; and it's your choice. What d'you think, Rosie?"

She was appealing to me, and I said, "I think you're right, Miss Clarke. I would like that better than starting in the big school straight away. It would be a sort of breaking-in period." And Miss Clarke went on to tell my dad about Miss Barrington. And he asked her where all this would take place. And she said, "Well, it would be up to you: she can either visit your house each day, or your daughter could visit hers, you live quite near each other as it happens. I myself think it would be better if Rosie were tutored at home. Have you a room that could be turned into a study?"

'Dad was smiling now and he repeated, "A room that could be turned into a study? There's a great big nursery on the second floor. That's where I spent my first years. It would be the very place for a schoolroom."

'"Well, in that case," said Miss Clarke, "perhaps you would like to meet her tomorrow and discuss the matter. Shall I arrange for her to come to your home?"

'"You can do that, by all means," he said. "And tomorrow afternoon will suit me fine."

'By that time, Mrs C, you can imagine I was bursting inside. I was wanting to break in with one of my . . . well, what you would call pieces of my repertoire. That would be the name for them, wouldn't it, Mr C?'

'Yes, Rosie,' Fred laughed; 'that's the name for them, your repertoire.'

'Well, to cut another long story short, Gran said it would be wonderful to have somebody upstairs again. Anyway, come the next day, there we were waiting for Miss Barrington; and when the front door was opened for her and she stood in the hall and we looked at each other, a funny thing happened. You know how it is, Mrs C, sometimes: you know when a thing is right or wrong, something inside tells you. And this tall woman, 'cos she was tall – she is tall – she's all of five foot nine or ten, well, we looked at each other, as I said, and something happened between us. I didn't know then what she thought about this individual who was staring at her, but I know now she felt the same as I do. And it's wonderful. Life's wonderful. Oh, you've got no idea.'

'No, we haven't any idea,' put in Fred, 'unless you're going to tell us about it. You're wasting phone time, do you know that? Your granny must be swimming in money to pay for these phone calls.'

'Aye, she is; and so is me dad, and he doesn't

mind. So what d'you think about that, Mr C?'

'No matter what Mr C thinks about it,' Sally put in, 'get on with it, Rosie. Tell us what happened next.'

'Well, everybody was introduced to everybody else. Then Dad and Miss Barrington and me went upstairs. In the nursery she stood looking round, and then, nodding her head, she said, "This will do splendidly. But it's a very cold room; you'll need central heating up here."

'Me dad stared at her. "Well, we always had fires on," he said.

'"That might have been so in your day, Mr Stevenson" – she smiled at him – "but today I don't think any member of any staff will relish carrying buckets of coal up here and cinders down."'

'"Aye," me dad nodded at her; "I see what you mean." And then she said, "I notice you have central heating downstairs; it would be quite a small job to extend it up here, because it's here your daughter and I will be from nine until twelve and from two until four each day. And one cannot take in much learning if one's teeth are chattering." We exchanged smiles; then looking about her again, she said, "We'll need a decent table and two chairs with padded backs. Perhaps you have another attic with odd pieces of furniture in it which might provide what we need."

' "There are no odd pieces of furniture in the attics up here, Miss Barrington," said me dad now. "But you've only to say what you want and you may have it."

' "Oh, that's nice to know, Mr Stevenson. Yes, indeed it is. Well, now that we are together, the three necessary people concerned in this affair, I think we should clarify exactly what is to be done." She looked from my father to me, then back to my father. "Your daughter will not, of course, need any uniform until she is ready for school, but I do think that part of her education should be given over to what she needs by way of ordinary clothes." This, Mrs C,' added Rosie now, 'made me open my eyes, as I hadn't imagined clothes having any part in my education; it was my mind I was worried about, not the things I was wearing. But Miss Barrington apparently didn't see it like this and so she put it plainly to Dad: "I think during the refining period," she said, "she should be given some idea of what is necessary in the way of dress for . . . well, different occasions."

'Dad stared at her. "Is she expected to go to balls?" he asked.

'Miss Barrington now laughed outright and said, "Not through me, Mr Stevenson, not through me; but I know one or two shops that would dress her nicely and give her discreet advice on what to wear, say, for outdoors or going to the theatre or for travelling or whatever she might be wanting to do in the future. It might cost money . . ."

'Again Dad put in here, "Well, I've already told you, whatever you need, up here, or for her in any way, you have a free hand."

'At this, Miss Barrington put her head back and laughed. And then, looking at Dad, she said, "Oh, you know, Mr Stevenson, there is nothing I like more than spending other people's money and buying things for which I know I shall not be expected to pay."

'Dad stared at her slightly open-mouthed as she went on, more calmly now and quietly, "But don't worry, as the weather gets colder, I shan't be pushing in a mink coat for myself."

'Now Dad actually laughed. I've never seen him for a long time so happy-looking and open-faced.'

There was a pause, and Fred said, 'Well, go on, tell us what he said to her.'

'Well, he said, "You know, Miss Barrington, I think I might draw the line at the mink coat. A good winter one, yes, or possibly something else might take your fancy, but not a mink coat."'

We were laughing now, but Rosie's voice had no laughter in it as she said, 'Believe me, Mr and Mrs C, I stood there dumbstruck. I couldn't have been more surprised. This was the woman who was going to teach me English or French or German or whatever and make me ready to be a lady, and there was me dad backchatting her, and they were both enjoying themselves. I could see they were. Then she turned to my father and said, "Would you mind leaving me with your daughter for a time, Mr Stevenson? We shall have a lot to discuss, and we want to get down to business as soon as possible, don't we?"

'And at this he nodded and said, "Yes. Yes, Miss Barrington; you're right. And I've got to get back to work too."

'When we were alone we stood looking at each other, and she said, "I must warn you, Rosie, that your path for the next few months is not going to be easy. You will be bored to death with repetition; you will get so sick of reading."

'"Oh, no, I won't!" I put in here. "I love reading. And I have a good memory. I can remember a full page of anything I've just read, and I can nearly give you word for word of a conversation." And she said, "Oh, can you? Well, that will help, but it will not minimise the work that lies before you. You still have to be ground in the crucible of English grammar."

'Aye, that's the words she used, I remember them: crucible of English grammar. "You have a very steep mountain to climb," she said, "because you haven't been born to it, but have come upon it at this age, and you will probably say to yourself, if I've been over this once I've been over it fifty times. But I can promise you one thing. Once you have climbed to the top of your mental mountain, you will see a horizon lit by the beauty of the English language, developed from the Anglo-Saxon and aided and abetted by Latin and French, and you will be amazed."

'Anyway, she held out her hand and took one of mine between her own two, and she patted it, saying, "I'm throwing you in at the deep end, but one day you'll thank me. And when our six months is up you mightn't want it to end there, you might wish it to go on for a year or more, and if that were the case, I should be delighted. And I know Miss Clarke would be too, because we both know you are a girl of intelligence beyond your age and background. I speak plainly to you now because I know you under-stand."

'And at this I looked up into her face. I knew my eyes were shining and that I was near to tears as I said, "Yes, Miss Barrington, I understand what you are saying."'

The Carpenters were standing very close together now and Fred took his wife's hand, for she was actually crying; and he, she could see, was full of emotion, as he said quietly over the phone, 'Rosie, you're a most unusual girl. Everything that teacher said is true. You have intelligence, high intelligence, yes, seemingly above your age, but not necessarily, I would say, above your background; and some day you will be somebody. Yes, you will be somebody.'

'Oh, Mr C. If only I had your shoulder here it would be wringing wet. Well, I must really go now, but before I do, a lot of other things have happened since Tuesday. I have learned a lot about Miss Barrington from Miss Collins, who is about the same age as Miss Barrington, and although she has never known her personally she knew about her. She was seventeen and engaged to a captain during the First World War, and just before the end of it he came home. He was just slightly wounded and everybody really thought the war was over, all but the signing, so they were married. Two days later he was sent back to France, and it must've been just hours before the last shot was fired that he was killed, shot by a sniper, he and three of his men. In 1919 she had a baby that came before its time and it died, and she nearly died too. She had a sort of breakdown. After she recovered she went to university, and later became a teacher. She lived with her parents until they died, but now she lives in a small flat quite near here. And what I have gathered during the last three days, in spite of her knowledge and her travelling abroad each year and so on, is that she is a lonely woman. Gran guessed this too, and so arrangements have been made that she has lunch with us and tea after she finishes at four. We have known her for such a short time but she seems to have fallen into our ways, I mean Gran's ways, not mine' – she laughed here – 'and she feels at home. I know she does.

'Oh, Mr and Mrs C, I wish you were nearer and I could come and talk to you. There's so much I want to say, and as yet I can't say it to anybody but you two. In fact, I don't think I'll ever be able to talk to anybody like I do to you, because you saw me in the raw. Oh, there are lots of things Miss Barrington has said to me. It is somehow like listening to you, Mr C, you know.

'Gran's just yelled up if I don't get off this phone she'll come and brain me and tell you she's gonna send you the bill; and she says when are you coming down to see her 'cos she wants to know what you look like? I'll have to say bye-bye now, dears; but, oh, if you could only see me you'd both go cock-eyed at the sight. Bye-bye, dears. Bye-bye.'

'Bye-bye, my love,' Sally said softly.

'Bye-bye, Rosie of the River,' Fred shouted.

'What did you say?'

'I said "Rosie of the River" because that's how we'll always think of you. Bye-bye, love.'

They didn't go back into the study but went into the kitchen, and when Sally stood quiet, with her hands lying flat on the table, he placed his arm around her shoulder, saying, 'What is it?'

'Oh, Fred, I've wished so often that we had had children to fill up this great cold house, and I can't help thinking that when I had those two miscarriages after we were first married one of them might have grown up to be like Rosie. It would have been the most wonderful thing that could have happened. In fact, now it seems an answer to a prayer that she's come into our lives just at this moment.'

'You're right there. She says we've done a lot for her, to help her get started on a new life. I don't suppose she's even thought that she might have done just as much for us in quite a different way.'

6

They heard nothing further from Rosie for a week, when a postcard from her set them thinking. It read:

> *So very busy, loves, upstairs and down. Gran has had a bad cold. James Watson would like to see you. Got in touch. Called here. Be phoning you. So much to say. Why don't you live near? Love to the three of you.*
>
> *Rosie*

When Fred came in from school, Sally passed the card to him and said, 'What do you make of that? James Watson would like to see us. Why didn't he phone?'

'I don't recall giving him our number,' said Fred.

'Well, he's been to see Rosie; she could have.'

'Well, we must wait and see, mustn't we?' said the schoolmaster. Then he added, 'How was work today?'

'Could be worse. I like the new winter stock I ordered. Some of it came in today, and it made me feel that we're beginning to throw off all the shortages and austerity we've had since the war. I think sales are picking up too.'

'Good.' He put his arm round her, kissed her, then said, 'Don't lose interest here, will you? Don't forget there isn't only dry rot and wood-worm to be seen to, there are seventeen leaks in that roof now; and the guttering on the far side is giving way. And what is more, we want to think about a trip abroad; or, like Mr Fawcett, we could think about buying a new boat.'

She gave him a gentle push. 'Before we come to the trip abroad or buying a new boat, I want some new clothes, I haven't had any for ages. If this new stock attracts more customers, I want – I've got to be at least as well dressed as they are.'

'There's always Mr Fawcett's silk stockings.'

'Huh! Those, as you know, are for special oc-casions, such as when the size of my orders is so big that I'm invited up to London to meet the manufacturers and attend all the major dress shows.'

Isn't it strange how things said in jest often take place in real life later on?

They hadn't long to wait to know what Rosie's postcard was all about, because that evening James Watson telephoned.

'Hello there,' he said. 'This is James Watson here.'

'And not before time,' Sally said; 'it's a fortnight since we waved goodbye.'

'Mrs C, I've been in jail for the past two weeks – well, I might as well have been – but on Friday coming, as never was, I'm being let out of the college until the Monday, and as usual I'm staying at the Rectory in London. Now, I know it's a two-hour or more journey from your country mansion up to the East End of London, but if you can join us next Saturday, I will meet you at the station and take you to the Rectory and present you to my papa and mama. Then you can hear what has happened in the last two weeks, or three, let's say . . . not to me, but to our friend, Pontoon Mouth. Remember him?'

Fred, who by now was standing by his wife's side, said, 'I'm here too, James. How are you?'

'Fine. Fine. Oh, it'll be good to see you both again. Anyway, as I said, you'd like to know what happened to Pontoon Mouth, wouldn't you?'

'We would. We would.'

'Well, I can tell you both, you're in for a surprise. That, though, I'll leave to my father because he was the executor of it all. I think he could have run the resistance in France during the war, the things he gets up to. Anyway, how are you really, both of you?'

'Oh, we're fine,' said Fred.

'And your back?'

'Oh, that's at its normal best. I can now fell a tree, and saw it up so that we don't freeze to death in this mausoleum of ours. By the way, you saw Rosie. How is she?'

'Oh, our Rosie. Well, she has fallen on her feet. You'll never believe it when you see her. Well, she's changed outwardly, her dress and her hairstyle and whatnot; but inwardly though, I fear, she is much the same. But she's living a different life. You must go and see her. The granny's got a lovely house, and it seems full of nice people. And this Miss Barrington is a gem. How she came across her I'll never really know, except I gather that you, Fred, had a hand in it.

Our Rosie is going places; I'm sure of that. But listen, can you come on Saturday?'

They looked at each other and Fred nodded. 'Well, it just happens that I do have next Saturday off. You see, normally we work on a Saturday morning, and only half a day on Wednesday. Yes; yes, of course we'll be there; we'll get the nine o'clock train from here. But there'll be three of us, as you know.'

'You're not bringing that dog of yours with you, surely? Don't forget, my mother has a bulldog.'

'Yes, I remember,' Sally said, and added, 'but we come with Bill or not at all.'

'Well, well! I suppose he'll have to. How is the old fellow?'

'Still lovely, and looking beautiful as always.'

'Well, until Saturday then, folks.'

'Until Saturday, James. Bye-bye.'

There he was, on the platform, waiting for them. He held out both arms towards them, and they greeted him like a long-lost friend. Then he was stooping over Bill and being kissed liberally.

'Oh, it's good to see you both,' he said. 'Had a good journey up?'

'Very good. We had one of those corner end

compartments, you know, that take two passengers only; and this suited us, His Nibs more so' – Fred pointed down at Bill – 'for he nearly always ends up in the guard's van; we two with him.'

James hustled them along to the queue waiting for the taxis. When Bill sniffed at the ankles in front of him there was some shuffling and moving to the side, and Sally had to say, 'He's quite harmless; he is really. Believe me.'

'That's after the stitches come out,' said the man next to the shuffling lady, and he laughed. The Carpenters did, too, but not so the lady. She got into the next taxi with an alacrity that gave the lie to her sixty years or more.

It took them thirty minutes to reach their destination. The Rectory was number twenty-four in a long, forbidding and dilapidated terrace; but once inside the linoed hall, the welcome they received from the man almost a head taller than his son was overwhelming. He was enormously tall and thin, and his wife, not half his height but three times as broad, greeted them with the same affectionate enthusiasm. The parson, smiling all over his face, talked all the time, saying, 'This is a day and a half. If only Peter had been able to come along. It's much warmer in the kitchen, but she will have us go into the sitting room which is heated only for weddings, funerals and baptisms, and none of those has happened in the family for many a long year.'

'Shut up, Sandy, and let's get in there and near the fire; they're frozen!'

'Oh! Isn't he beautiful?' She was bending down to Bill who, now that he was off the leash, was attempting to find out exactly where he was and whom he might meet by sniffing into the corners.

'Where's Princess, Mother?' James asked her.

'Oh, she's next door, with the Brownlows. You know how they love her. We thought, as we were having a gentleman to visit us' – she was now stroking Bill – 'who was a very strong and fine chap, it would be a bit too exciting, for nowadays our dear Princess's legs give way under a puff of wind.' And she looked up at Sally as she said, 'We had a bull terrier once, called Macnab.' She glanced up at the tall figure now ushering them towards a door at the end of the hall.

It was noticeable that neither of the Carpenters had had a chance to get a word in, not even when they were settled in what was really a very cosy room and in front of a roaring fire. In fact, there had fallen on the company a short silence, until the little woman said, 'Now we've all got our breath back, how are you, my dears?'

From then the conversation was general until Mrs Watson said, 'I'm not going to say I hope you don't mind eating in the kitchen, because that's where we always eat, that is if there's anything left in the larder. More often than not Sandy's already been there and taken it out for somebody he says needs it more than we do, when I have to say to him, "You speak for yourself, Sandy Watson."'

It struck Sally, at this moment, that if Mrs Watson had been Rosie's granny she would have recognised her as one of the Stevenson family, but she wasn't Rosie's granny. Quite by chance, she was an elderly, grown-up Rosie.

Apparently her husband hadn't got his hands on today's meal for it was very good. It started with a home-made broth which, Mrs Watson informed them as she placed steaming bowls on the table, was called Watson's Saviour. It had been made from a stock of ham bones and shin bones and pigs' trotters, together with a basis of well-cooked barley and vegetables, the main ingredient here being leeks.

It was the finest broth Fred and Sally had ever tasted. As Sally was telling her that, or trying to, Sandy put in, 'Why don't you come out with that pud of yours?'

'Shut up!' had been her reply to him. 'And get that broth down that drainpipe first 'cos, if you don't, when you're found dead I'll get the blame of it . . . malnutrition, it will be said.'

James had kept smiling all through this family repartee, occasionally casting his glance towards the Carpenters and shaking his head at the same time, as much as to say, 'You've heard nothing yet'. And it was true. Those two could have filled any theatre with their natural back-chat. That afternoon the Carpenters laughed more than they could remember ever doing before. But then, it was not difficult after a very good meal of roast lamb and four vegetables and a pudding, a beautiful Yorkshire pudding sprinkled with raisins, sultanas and currants, topped with a brandy sauce, the spirit in which, Mrs Watson assured them, was no imitation but was from a miniature bottle that had been given to her for medicinal purposes.

They had arrived at the Rectory at about a quarter past twelve, but it was turned two before they went back into the sitting room; and there, of a sudden, the little woman's manner changed: turning to her husband, who was sitting in a large well-worn leather chair to the side of the fireplace opposite her, she said, 'Well, now, Sandy. No more fumblegilgoosling, but let's talk sensibly for the next while and tell them about Charles, because, really, that's why they're here today, to find out about Charles.'

'Oh, no,' Fred put in gallantly; 'not only to find out about Charles, we wanted to meet you too.'

'Thank you, Mr Carpenter,' said the little woman. 'That's very nice of you. But now, sit back and listen to him giving you preliminary details before he takes you on a journey, and what a journey, you'll find. James and I will sit before this fire and wait for you to come back, by which time somebody will have got a decent tea set in the kitchen. That's if there's anything there and I empty his pockets before he goes out. Now on with it, Sandy.'

The Reverend Watson looked from one to the other of his audience, then said quietly to Fred, 'You've met Mr Charles McHannen?'

'No. Not exactly. We didn't really meet him, though we certainly heard him, and from a distance we saw him twice in the boat and once standing on the top of a sand dune on Breydon Water; but we never really met him.'

'Well, as for me,' began Sandy Watson again, 'he was introduced to me by two worried young men who were about to go on a sailing trip across the Broads. They had met up with this man, an American with whom they had been rather friendly at university. And so, coming to England, he looked them up again, only to find out he was about to lose them because they were going on a trip. So he put it to them that he would like to join them. Neither of them was eager for his company, but what could they do?

'They both agree it isn't Charlie's own fault that he is loud-mouthed, utterly selfish, and with the idea that money can buy everything. He has plenty of that, or at least his father has and what his father has is his because his father adores him, so we are given to understand. Yet his father sees that his valet-cum-guardian and spy watches his every move and reports them back to him. Knowing on which side his bread is buttered, the valet does as he is told, even though I'm sure he aims to twist his reports just slightly to show that the boss's son is behaving himself. You see, Charles had left New York under a cloud. As I understand it, Mr Charles McHannen had a friend whose name was whisky, and when under his friend's control he always sang long and loudly. So wherever he went he was an embarrassment, and Peter and James here, I think, had had enough when they at last left him on the Wednesday of your holiday and came to me. And so' – he spread out his hands – 'here were the two of them, when the impression they gave me was here was a man spending money like water on whisky and debauchery of every form and kind and not giving a thought, not even a damn' – his voice rose as he said the last word – 'not even a *damn* on how the other half existed. He didn't even know there was another half. If he had thought, he would have said, "Well, what are they but servants? They are paid for being servants; let them get on with it! I live my life and they live theirs. What the hell!"'

Sally and Fred were fascinated. This wasn't the funny, jovial man of a couple of hours ago, this was a clergyman who was using ordinary language, very ordinary language. Rosie . . . Oh, Rosie would have loved him.

'It came to my mind,' went on the Reverend Watson, 'that there was no-one so bad that they couldn't be made a little better if their eyes were opened to the truth, and the plot that these two young fellows had put before me seemed to be possible but, as they said, they couldn't do it without my help. What would I suggest? I took a few minutes over the matter before I said, 'Well, if you intend to get him so blotto that he'd have passed out, he'll have a hangover for a couple of days, and if he finds himself without clothes and having to stay in some hole or other in this part of the city I can't think of anybody better than the Connollys for carrying out your plan. No; nor a more cold, bare house in which to wake up and learn there is a different kind of life from that which he has been leading. And they both said, "Fine. Fine." And then they asked how long I could keep him there – or the Connollys could keep him there. Well, I said it all depended on how long it would take the cleaner to get the mud and filth off that suit after they had dipped him here and there in the gutters, as they had proposed, the scheming rats that they were.'

His head bowed, his lips tight-closed in an effort to check his laughter, James made no response, and his father went on: 'I was left holding the baby. How was I expected to deal with what followed?

'What I gathered, in bits and pieces, would fill a book but nobody would believe it. One incident young Willie Connolly told me of was, when he himself was getting up early in the morning from the pallet on which he had been lying on the floor to go to his paper round, the man lying in the bed croaked, "Get me a drink." And Willie said, "Get it yourself, there's a mug on the chair beside you," which seemed to bring the fellow to life and he croaked again, "Where am I then?"

'"With us, the Connollys," Willie said.

'"Look, get me a drink," the man said, "I don't want water, I want a drink."

'"Well, you'll have to wait for ten minutes; Mattie's just brewed, and it's on the hob. She always likes it strong."

'And when the man said, "Turn the light on," Willie answered him, "I can't, that costs money. Anyway it's daylight now. When I get into me things I can pull the curtains."

'"Into your things?" the man repeated. "Where have you been sleeping? In this bed?"

'"No, I haven't been sleeping in the bed. On

191

the mattress where I usually sleep at the foot."

'Again the fella sits up, said Willie, and said, "Where on earth am I? Get who's in charge. Who owns this place?"

' "You'll hear who's in charge if you yell like that, and that'll be from me dad." '

Here the clergyman looked from one to the other of his listeners. 'I can imagine Willie's voice rising and explaining emphatically, "And we don't want any pity; we're quite happy, thank you." He is a proud boy, and clever too . . . No; you couldn't find a happier family. God knows how they manage. But in spite of all, they're happy.'

He laughed now as he went on, ' "Get the girl to come up here," Charles demanded of Willie.

' "I'd say to you, sir, if you had any clothes to put on," answered Willie, "get her yerself. And if you spoke to her like that you'd get yer answer, I can tell you. You've got to be very careful how you speak to Mattie; she's got a head on her shoulders." And Charles's immediate reaction to this was to bawl, "I don't care where the hell her head is, get her up here. I want to know what's going on."

' "You'll know soon enough." Yes, that's what the boy replied, for at that moment the door opened and there stood Mattie with a mug of tea in her hand; and she looked at our dear Charles and said, "What're you yelling at? You've woken my dad up, and my mum too, and she's only just got off to sleep. Now, there's a cup of tea. There's no sugar in it; we're out of that at the moment; but it's strong."

'Charles did not take the mug from her but stared at her; then he must have forced himself to speak civilly, for he said, "Would you tell me what all this is about, please?"

' "Yes, if you want to know. But take this mug unless you want me to take it back again."

'After Charles had taken the mug from her she said, "Our neighbour next door came and said there was a corpse lying in the gutter outside. He had seen two fellas dropping it there. He wanted to ask my dad if he would get the police, because he had been in trouble with them himself. And my dad yelled, "No! Get Willie to help you carry him in." They carried you up here, and helped strip you of your filthy clothes before laying you on my bed. Yes, this is my bed. My mum took your vest and pants and washed them, but she couldn't wash the mud off your outer clothes, they would have to go to a cleaner's. Willie there" – she pointed to her brother – "put them in a sack and took them there yesterday."

'There she stopped, and Charles asked her quietly, "How long will that take?"

' "Don't ask me," Mattie replied. "I'm not a cleaner." Then when she asked, "Would you like me to get in touch with your family or friends? You must know someone in London, I suppose," he almost screamed back at her, "No! No! I'll wait for my clothes. I'll be all right." Then more quietly, "By the way, was there any money at all on me?"

' "No, not a farthing. But don't worry, we won't charge you much. We live cheaply here. And you should thank your stars you *are* here, because if the police had been called you would have been in clink by now. Just think on that. And you would have had to get in touch with your people, wouldn't you? Well, the quicker you do, in any case, the better I'll like it, because as I said this is my bed. By the way, there's no bathroom here, you'll empty your own slops from under the bed into the bucket that's been placed for you in the cubby-hole outside the door there. You'll see it all right, there's no other door on the landing. Willie will empty it for you."

'On this, Willie said she turned to him and

194

said quietly, "You'd better put a move on, Willie, it's close on seven o'clock."'

Sandy Watson now stretched out his hands to the fire, saying, 'There you have a picture of the awakening of our dear Charles at the beginning of the plot.'

Sally looked at James and said, 'You said that's what you came to London to do that day, wasn't it? You said you were plotting something.'

'Yes, we worked it all out on that Wednesday and we carried it out on the Friday and, oh, I never felt so sorry for anyone in my life as when we left Charlie at the Connollys' door, at least I should say in the gutter. But it's amazing what's happened since. It is really, isn't it, Father?'

Sandy Watson said, 'Indeed it is, son. Indeed it is. God works in strange ways.' And he paused before he added, on a laugh, 'Even through men with little brain.'

At this point, it was Mrs Watson who said, 'I'd say it's about time you were off, if you want to show them anything in the daylight. And don't forget, Sandy, you're taking a parcel to the Connollys' today.'

'Oh, that's something I won't forget, dear. No, I won't forget that.'

Just as they were about to leave the house Mr Watson took his son aside and said, 'Stay with your mother, son. If you come with us, she won't sit there just stroking the dog all the time, she'll be busying herself remembering that tomorrow you'll be going away again and she won't see you for months. Sit with her, would you?'

'Yes, Father; oh, yes, I'd like nothing better; I just thought you might want me to come along with you.'

They nodded at each other and the clergyman opened the door for the Carpenters so that they could begin their walk through the East End of London.

They were in a district which seemed to be the slummiest of slums and damaged by wartime bombing: up narrow alleys, where the smell would have knocked you down, where sounds of laughter, crying and yelling came from different houses; some children playing outside looked so drab and dirty they might not have seen water for years.

Eventually, they left the huddle of buildings to emerge into a clearer area in which the houses were terraced, but still so dilapidated and unkempt, again partly due to bomb damage, it was impossible to imagine anyone living in them.

During their walk and Sandy Watson's description of each part they were passing through, Sally noticed he was coughing and that it was a hard, tight cough. Once or twice she said to him, 'Are you all right?' and he replied, 'Right as rain, my dear. Right as rain.' That was, until they came to an open area which he told them was used as a market on certain days of the week. In one corner was a public house: the sign above the doors read: 'The Last Rung of the Ladder'. It was here that, surprisingly, the clergyman stopped and said, 'Would you mind if we called in here for a moment? We'll be able to sit down and talk, and I should like to tell you the rest before we get to the Connollys'.' He was wheezing now as he led them up a back alley and through a door into a small room. A man appeared behind a lift-up counter, and cried 'Well! Hello, Reverend! Hello! Isn't this a day for the Church; I've just had Father Mackin in. Oh, it's good to see yourself. It's very rare you visit us; it's mostly your grand lady I see.'

'Hello, Sammy. Would your snug be quiet about this time?'

'As quiet as the grave, sir. And if it's not I'll make it so for you. Come through. Come through.' He lifted the flap of the counter and the others followed through into a narrow passage lined with barrels, then into a small room, which also had a flap counter. Leather seats lined two walls, and there was a small round iron table between them. Here the publican cried, 'Sit yourselves down. Sit yourselves down.'

'Has my good lady been bothering you of late, Sammy?'

'I haven't seen her, Reverend, for some time. But bothering me? It's a delight to see her. I tell you I have never seen that bar, full of men, laugh so much as when she pushes through them. The last time she came in she had them roaring, and, I can tell you, to the amazement of the new customers because, as you know, that big room is for men only. But there she was, pushing up to the counter where I could just see her head above it and she said to me for everybody to hear, "Sammy, would you be after having a few drops of that whisky that you keep back from their glasses when serving customers? Just a few drops would do." And I answered her, "I have the very thing, Mrs Watson, the very thing. It's been waiting for you. Is it your husband's chest again?"

'"It's not only his chest," she said; "it's every other part of him. He's coughing down to his toenails."

'"You should have heard that bar! And you know, they all wanted to stand her drinks. Yes, they did. I could've made nigh a fortune that day if she had only said, "I won't have it now, but if you leave the money I'll have them later." You know what she said to them on that day? "Thank you all very much. It's most kind of you, but if I was to touch the stuff it would go straight to my head and I would be apt to say strange things and do stranger things still, and the good Lord knows what Sandy would do if they locked me up." And some bloke cried at her, "Who's Sandy, ma'am?" and when she replied, "My husband, the Reverend Philip Watson, minister of this parish," they actually fell about. They didn't believe a word she was saying. I couldn't get them to believe it until she had gone out, and you know what she went out saying?'

'No; but I have a good idea, Sammy.'

'Well, Reverend, she went out saying, "You are the most Christian heathen I know, Sammy. And you know something else? There are more

Christians among the non-believers than the believers themselves." That's what she said.'

After Sammy had laughed loudly and Mr Watson, smiling, had nodded his confirmation of the statement, Sammy said, 'What would you all like to drink?'

At this, Fred put in, 'If you don't mind I'd like to see to the drinks.'

'Not while you're in the company of the Reverend, you won't, sir. I very rarely see him, and when I do he is my guest and whoever is with him. Now tell me what you would like? Madam?'

'Oh, thank you, Mr . . .'

'Just call me Sammy, ma'am. Just call me Sammy.'

Sally laughed. 'Well, Sammy, I'd like a sherry.'

'And you, sir?' He now turned to Fred.

'A shandy, if you wouldn't mind, Sammy.'

'I wouldn't mind in the least. And for my dear friend, the usual hot toddy? And I'll see to it myself now.'

'He's a good man,' said Mr Watson; 'none better. You know, every year he collects from all his customers in order that I might have parcels to send to all those in need, parcels as well as clothes dockets. He often collects a great deal of money, but he has to smile when I say to him, "The same rule stands, Sammy?" and he says, "It's all right with me, Reverend." And my rule is, you know, that I don't give any of my parishioners a present in actual money, because I know that the women would see very little of it, while the men would be in this bar or another spending every penny that they have. It's a strange life, isn't it? And Sammy laughs about the arrangement where many another so-called Christian publican would not.

'But now, I must quickly put you in the picture of what happened next. I'll have to make it short.

'After three days in that room and not a drop of whisky, mind, and meals that he himself would not have given to a stray dog, Charles consents to go down into the living room. He had been given an outsize overcoat from Paddy's market, as well as a pair of cloth slippers, which were too small for him. By this time the poor fellow was almost out of his mind and continually asked if someone would find out if his clothes had been cleaned, only to be told simply that the cleaner was doing his best with them.

'What really made him make a move was when Mattie came into his room, accompanied by Willie, who was carrying a tin dish of hot water, and she had a cut-throat razor and a saucer on which was soap and a shaving brush with her. "What's that for?" his lordship had enquired apprehensively. And Mattie had answered, "I'm going to give you a shave."

'"By God, you're not!" Charles had bawled. "This is the limit. Are you all mad here?" But Mattie went on, calmly for her, "I'll not cut your throat. I shave me dad every week, and I've left no scars on him. And you look terrible. D'you know that?"

'I understand Charles was about to protest physically when she pushed a brushful of soap almost into his mouth, and within seconds had lathered his face. Then gripping his nose, she said, "You remain still and I'll not leave a mark on you."'

Here Sandy Watson took a drink of his hot toddy, while his shoulders shook. Then he said, 'Charlie himself has told me since that his eyes must have seemed to be popping out of his head, and he couldn't believe it when she finally dipped the corner of a rough towel into the warm water and wiped his face clean, and it really did feel good. He didn't thank her, but just gaped at her.

'Apparently her last words were: "Now to meet me dad and without scaring me mum."

'He told me that downstairs he was further amazed at the poverty of the room: a table, four small chairs, a wooden settee with a thin padded cover; but what struck him straight away was the basket chair on which a man was sitting propped up.

'He was introduced to this man, Joe, and to his wife Ada. But it was a long and embarrassing silence before another word was spoken, when Joe said, "I'm sorry about your clothes, sir. They shouldn't be long now . . . Do you play cribbage, sir?"

'Reluctantly, Charles admitted he could play. And that's how the rest of the evening and the next day were passed. And yet all the while Charles was taking in, and not without some horror, the way these people existed; and from the talk that went on, seemingly better than some in the same street and district.

'His mind must have been in a desperate state when he thought of me. We hadn't met, but he knew that James's father was a parson somewhere in the East End. And so he asked Joe if he knew of a parson named Watson, which, of course, he did.'

He finished his drink and leaned back saying, "I knew how Judas felt at the Last Supper when Charles greeted me in his bedroom almost with open arms, then poured out his plight. Could I help him in any way? He did not wish his father to find out what had happened to him."

'I realised he had no memory whatsoever of his last meeting with James and Peter, except that they'd had a farewell supper together.

'It was then I knew that this farce couldn't go on. The idea had been to make him aware of how the other half lived, hoping it would bring to the fore the better side of him. Well, I knew then that he had already experienced more than enough, and that from then on only time would tell whether or not the boys' intention had succeeded.

'They had meant that he should be taken to Paddy's market to be rigged out and to become acquainted in some way with the McTaggarts, an Irish family of ten, living further down the street in dire poverty. But I decided, no; no more; that mustn't happen. The poor fellow had had enough. And so I promised I would go myself to the cleaner's and see about his clothes.

But then there was the further matter of his shoes, which were missing. What I suggested was that I should go out and buy a pair of very ordinary ones, but that the money would have to be taken out of the church fund, which I was sure he would not mind replenishing.

'It took another day before this was all accomplished. It was his fifth day with the Connollys. However, before he said goodbye to them by thanking them very warmly, he made a surprising request of me: would I hire a taxi and go home with him and there explain to his man that he'd had a fall and had been staying with me because I was his friend's father?'

Again Mr Watson laughed and dolefully shook his head. 'Well I had told so many lies of late, what did another matter? Although this one was a whopper, which would have to be handled tactfully.'

'What did his man say?' Fred asked. 'How was he greeted?'

'In one way, with relief, because he wouldn't now have to phone Charles's father and confess that he had lost sight of his beloved son for almost a week. On the other hand he showed utter disbelief of my story, because there was his master in the stained suit, which had shrunk, and a pair of cheap shoes, looking as though he hadn't been to his barber for days.

'Charles begged me to stay and have a bite with him somewhere, but would I excuse him until he had changed?'

Again Sandy Watson's shoulders were shaking as he said, 'I could hear the bath-water running, poor fellow. I was glad his man was upstairs with him, for had he started grilling me, I feel I would have been unable to match him.

'Well, the dear fellow took me out to lunch, not in a smart place, nevertheless a nice restaurant. And I must admit to enjoying a meal as I hadn't had for a long time, simply, as my good woman said later, because this time I couldn't push it into my pocket. And a surprising thing happened at that meal and I cannot say if it foretells good or not. The waiter brought a wine list, and I realised Charles was looking at it without reading it. Perhaps I was expecting him to say, "Bring me a whisky"; instead, it was a red burgundy, and, I knew, a good one.

'After our glasses had been filled, he looked down into his, then sipped at it as if he had never before tasted wine. When he laughed, I joined him, although I didn't know what he was actually laughing at, until he said: "Five full days on water and boiled tea. I should be gobbling this up, shouldn't I? But I've never been keen on wine, although I have drunk it with meals since I was five years old, when my father insisted that I should eat with him. As you must know by now, whisky is my drink. And you know, Parson, I'm afraid now to see it, or even smell it. Whatever happened to me the other night when I was blotto and was picked up out of the gutter by the kind Connollys has made me realise how far one can sink through that particular drink. I have always imagined I could carry it; but it carried me into the gutter. Consequently, being unable to get any more of the dog that bit me, as the saying goes, I have been compelled to do some thinking. The past five days have been like years during which I have seen myself as I never have before. Those people, their way of life, and that of all those around them, as Joe said, working their guts out to keep a roof over their heads and a bite in their belly, at least most of them. But then, they are probably an exceptional family, making the best of a bad job."

' "Will you go back to your favourite drink?" I dared to ask.

'He considered a moment before he said, "I don't know, sir. I only know this: strangely,

I now shall have the power to control my intake."

'After that day we saw each other a number of times, when he couldn't do enough for me. He has left a good sum for the Christmas boxes.'

'Has he gone then?' put in Fred quickly.

'Yes; he flew back yesterday, he and his man. He wants to take up a definite position in his father's business.'

And with this, Sandy Watson stood up, saying, 'Let's away then and deliver his message to the Connollys.'

They passed through another dingy street and finally came to a long road of run-down houses, when their guide said, 'We are almost there.'

Although the Carpenters had been given an idea of the living room and bedroom, their imaginations had not been able to provide a picture of what confronted them now. They had both been in poor houses before; Sally herself had been brought up in her grandmother's kitchen-cum-eating-and-sometimes-sleeping room after her mother's death, but never had she seen anything like this. The only thing she could say about it was that it was clean, but it was poverty at its lowest and barest. Yet the four people who greeted them were all bright-faced and lively. Even the man who lay in the basket chair had a wide smile on his pale face as he held out a crippled hand in greeting. His wife, too, welcomed them like part of the family who had just dropped in, and the boy, Willie, who seemed all arms and legs, laughed as he took Fred's hand, saying, 'Blimey, sir, I never thought I'd shake hands with a schoolmaster.' As for Mattie, the vixen, she was a very pretty soft-voiced girl of perhaps sixteen, not dissimilar to Rosie. Rosie was better formed, but in a way she had had every chance to be, for at least she had been well fed whereas this girl, to go by this room and what Mr Watson had spoken of, lived on bread and scrape a lot of the time.

'Sit down! Sit down!' cried Ada Connolly, pointing to the settle. 'Bring a chair up for His Reverence and place it near the fire,' she said to her son.

At this Mattie said, 'My mother means, Your Reverence, that you look half frozen.'

'Yes, I know she does, Mattie, while at the same time I'm aware the fire is pretty well lost on me because I always look half frozen. At least, that's what my wife tells me.'

They were all laughing now. Then it was the

man on the chair who spoke: 'Our friend has gone off back home, then, sir?' he said to the clergyman.

'Yes, Joe. Yes. He went off yesterday, but he'll be popping back and forth, I have no doubt.'

'You know, sir, I was sorry for him. It was all supposed to be a lark, as you said, but he must have gone through the mill.'

'Yes, you are right, Joe, you are right there. And my main purpose in coming here today, dear friends, is to bring you his thanks and this.' From the inside of his jacket he now pulled out a brown paper bag, and leaning towards the table, he extracted from it four letters and, in silence now, he handed, first, one to Ada; then one to Joe; the third he gave to Mattie; and the last to Willie; and he said, 'These are from your friend. He asked me to deliver them once he had left the country.'

They all looked down at the envelopes; then it was Mattie who said, 'Let me slit it open for you, Dad.' And taking a knife from the drawer at the end of the table, she slit the top of the envelope then handed it back to him. Out of it fell three pieces of paper. He laid them on the edge of the table. He picked up first the piece of white paper and read out the words that were written there: 'Joe, I always honour my gambling debts.' Then he picked up the second piece of paper, which he recognised: it was the scrap of paper on which he had written down what they had won or lost at their games of cards or cribbage. Then picking up the cheque, he held his other hand to his head as he cried, 'God Almighty! It was never meant. It wasn't; it was only a joke; in fun. Never in me life!' He now pushed the cheque towards his wife, and she read out slowly, 'To Joseph John Connolly, four hundred and forty-seven pounds,' and her exclamation was, 'Holy Mary, Mother of God!' She looked at her husband and he at her, and he shook his head as he said, 'It was never meant; it was all a joke, it was all a bit of fun.'

Quietly now, the clergyman put in, 'He wanted you to have it, Joe. He was so thankful for your company; he has told me so himself.'

'Open yours, Mother,' said Mattie now. She hadn't touched her own envelope; and with the same knife Ada slit hers open. She took out only two pieces of paper. She lifted one up and read, 'Dear Ada, This is for being a mother to me, something I never knew. Go to the agent named on the back of this page and he will give you the choice of a flat or small house. The enclosed cheque will help you to furnish it. I shall always be in your debt, dear Ada. Charles.'

The tears were now streaming down Ada's face; but when she lifted up the cheque she seemed to wail aloud like an animal, but not in pain, and she repeated, 'Five hundred pounds! Oh, Holy Mary! Holy Mary! Why is God being so good to us through that dear man?'

Mattie had by now opened her envelope, and from it she took a cheque and a piece of paper, and she too read aloud: 'To a little lady who played the part of vixen. But if she decides to take up barbering as a career she has only to let me know. The enclosed is for you to spend on yourself, and I repeat, on yourself, Mattie. We'll meet again some time and talk. Charles.'

Her face now running with tears, Mattie held up a cheque, muttering, 'A hundred pounds. A hundred pounds.'

All eyes were now turned on the boy. Willie had already opened his envelope and had read the note inside. He looked from one to the other and back to the sheet of paper, but for a moment could not force himself to speak. Then he read, 'You did my dirty work for me, Willie, and without a grumble. Get yourself some nice gear, and work hard at school. Stay there as long as you can, then go to a better one if you can; but whichever way your results show, there'll be a job waiting for you in our company. My thanks, Willie. Charles. And there's a cheque for a hundred pounds.'

Sally was seeing everything through a blur. There was Joe with his body twisted round on his chair, his elbows resting on the edge of the table and his face covered with his hands. There was Ada, her head lying on her folded arms, her body shaking, and there was Mattie sitting now on a stool beside her father's chair. Her head was bowed and one hand was pressed tightly across her jaws. As for the boy, he was standing against the fireplace wall to the side of Sandy Watson. His body looked limp, his arms were hanging slackly by his sides. His head was bent forward and kept nodding as if he were telling himself something, and he was making no effort to wipe the drops that were running off the end of his nose. As for Mr Watson, he too was full of emotion. This poor family had been given a gold mine, and all because they had fallen in with a silly plan that a young doctor and a budding priest had thought up in order to shock a man into seeing that there was another side of life other than the one he was leading.

The tall angular clergyman was sitting trying to warm his hands at the fire now in order to cover his feelings. For it was he, really, who had manoeuvred the whole thing and with the help of this family had made it possible. It said something, Sally thought, for Peter and James that they should have seen in their aggravating, loud-mouthed, unpopular associate something worth saving, something good beyond all the flamboyance, the heavy drinking, the loose women, the utter wantonness.

'Come on. Come on,' said Mr Watson. 'No more tears. This is supposed to be a joyful occasion. I'm sure Charles meant it to be.'

'Oh, yes, yes,' added Ada. 'God bless him this night and every day of his life. God bless him.'

She was cut off by her daughter suddenly crying, 'Mum! Mum! Listen to me, and listen carefully. Don't mention to Father Mackin anything about these gifts, or he'll have half of it off you and onto the plate or in some scheme he's got going. Now, listen, Mum. Do you hear me? I say it to you again now: you are not to mention this to Father Mackin.'

Before Ada could speak her father had put in, 'She's right. She's definitely right, Ada. He'd have half from each one of us and on the plate.

You know him. You should by now. Has he ever given us a penny for anything? But he sends messages, through Willie there, that they're collecting for this, that and the other; and what was the message last time? That God always gives back with interest whatever is given to him. And I see he was right in that, at least, because tonight we've been given back interest. But not through him.'

'Don't keep on,' Ada said. 'And don't think I'm a fool altogether, Joe. I know what Father Mackin's like, always have, not like the Reverend here, who sees we have a box every Christmas. And I'm not of his church, though Joe is. And yet we never cross your church door, do we, Reverend?'

'We wouldn't dare, would we, Reverend?' said Mattie, laughing towards the parson now. 'Father Mackin would have us hung, drawn and quartered.'

'He would that, Mattie. He would without a doubt,' said Sandy Watson, laughing back at her. 'It's as much as he can stand that I'm allowed in the house to see your father.'

Ada now looked towards their other visitors, and said, 'You must take us for a very funny lot, Mr and Mrs Carpenter.'

'What we take you for, Mrs Connolly,' said Fred, 'is a very brave woman, and it's wonderful to see life working out well for you all at last. We hope we shall have the pleasure of meeting up with you all again some time soon.'

What time they left that bare but happy room they couldn't remember. They only knew that when they got back to the vicarage there was a lovely tea waiting for them, and a very excited Bill, as well as James and his mother, who wanted to know all that had happened at the Connollys.

Many hours later, when they were home and in bed, which had been heated with hot-water bottles, the last words Sally said before she went into a deep sleep were, 'Isn't life wonderful?'

7

How many days was it? How many weeks ago was it? How many years ago was it since Sally had said, 'Isn't life wonderful?' Just now, she felt she must have been mad: life was never wonderful.

For some time she had been plagued by heavy nosebleeds in the wake of a bad cold, the house was colder than ever and, to cap it all, although trade had indeed picked up at the shop, the strain of coping with the increased business as well as everything else at home single-handed had left her depressed, worried and exhausted. And, as always at such time, memories of her lost babies would return, together with the knowledge that she and Fred had not been able to fill the empty rooms with the sound of children's voices.

Fred's love could do nothing to help her,

immersed as he was in school work, but she knew he was worried to death. At lunch-time, he would fly home from school and beg her to lie down. But no, her motto had always been 'work it off', and the big house needed that motto: it had to be spotless before she would allow herself to settle down in the evenings and at weekends. But the nosebleeds flowed so freely that it took all the strength from her; all she could do was plug her nose with cottonwool and lie still while waiting for it to cease.

And so it came to a Saturday afternoon in the drawing room, where Fred had her propped up comfortably in the corner of the big couch in front of a roaring fire. He had also made the tea, and there it was set out on a small table by her side.

She was beginning to feel better now and think how lucky she was to have someone like Fred, who always took such care of her at times like these.

As he poured out another cup of tea for her he said, 'Do you know where we were this time a month ago?'

She had to think for a moment, then said, 'The Connollys' kitchen.'

'Yes, the Connollys' kitchen, and the gold

mine Mr Watson brought in and the tears and the laughter. If it had been in a play you wouldn't have believed it.'

Suddenly, Sally said, 'Don't you think it's odd we haven't heard from Rosie for some weeks?'

'Yes and no. She'll be up to her eyes in work now that she's under Miss Barrington; and don't forget she's staying with her grandmother, and her father's bound to be there for two or three days in the week.'

It was just at that moment that the phone rang. During the past week they had had an extension taken into the drawing room to prevent having to jump up, it always seemed, immediately they had settled down in the evening. So now, all Fred did was reach out to a small table on which the extension stood and say, 'Yes, this is . . .' But before he was halfway through the voice came quite clearly into the room: 'May I speak to Mrs Carpenter, please?'

'Who's speaking?'

'Miss Collins. I am companion and help to Mrs Stevenson senior.'

He passed the receiver over to his wife.

'Oh, Miss Collins; this is Mrs Carpenter here. We were just talking about Rosie; I hope nothing's wrong.'

'Yes, I'm afraid there's a lot wrong, Mrs Carpenter; but not really with Rosie. Something very tragic could have happened. Fortunately it was prevented, but only just in time. She wanted you to know about it and asked me to ring you. I think I'd better start from the beginning. Have you a moment to listen?'

'Oh, yes; yes, of course. My husband is sitting near me: we are very anxious to know what has happened.'

'Well, I think you already know that Mr Stevenson is moving his work down to the south. He found a factory on a very good site; but it was much larger than his original one. However, he decided to take it and sell the one in Birmingham; and fortunately this was settled in a very short time. Well, last Wednesday he was saying goodbye to those of his workers who would not be coming south with him and had opened a few bottles of beer as a send-off. They were quite satisfied with the financial arrangements he had made, such as pensioning off the older ones and having made sure that the others would be kept on by the new firm who had bought the factory. Twelve of the single women staff were moving with him, as were the manager and the four department heads.'

It seemed that Miss Collins was pausing for breath, and Fred and Sally exchanged worried glances. Then the fluttering voice continued.

'So everything as you can imagine was very pleasant. Then after the workers had gone, the manager and the heads of department adjourned over the yard to the office to have a last word with Mr Stevenson, who, I understand, was walking through all the workshops as if saying his last goodbye to them. You see, the factory had been built by his great-grandfather towards the middle of the last century. However, instead of leaving it by the front door, he must have continued to the back of the building and left by the side door, because it was from outside that the men in the office heard the scream. They ran out and along the front of the building and up one side, but saw nothing until they came to the back and the open scrubland, across which two men were scrambling. Knowing the land was surrounded by a high wall, they went after the intruders, and there was much scuffling. But when at last they had the men firmly on the ground and it was obvious the blood on their hands and faces was connected with the cry they had heard, the police were sent for.

'It was almost dark, I understand, and the man who had been sent to ring for the police could have missed the body that was lying against one of the sheds had it not been for the snuffling of a stray dog. And there to his horror he saw his boss, the man who had shaken his hand only half an hour before while telling him what his position would be in the new firm. So he phoned not only the police but for an ambulance as well.'

Again Miss Collins paused for breath; then went on, 'It's another long story and I will cut it short. The men they found were two of the younger Mrs Stevenson's many nephews, and from the moment they were in the police station and being questioned they blurted out that it was Mrs Stevenson who had paid them to give her husband a 'going over'. That was the term they used, and I understand they had added that she herself meant them to murder her husband. She had paid them two hundred pounds each with more to follow, but they had both agreed that they weren't going to carry out her wishes; they would mess him up a bit – oh, yes, because they didn't like him themselves, they admitted – but murder was a different thing. They weren't going to swing for doing her dirty work.'

'But how is Mr Stevenson?' Fred put in impatiently.

'Well, Mr Carpenter, I'm glad to say not as bad as we thought at first. You see, his head was badly cut and both men said they never hit him on the head with anything. It was when they knocked him down that he must have fallen on a sharp-edged piece of stone because his skull was cracked. His body was in a state: he had two broken ribs and was badly bruised all over. He must have been kicked. His mother and Rosie sat in the hospital all during that first night; but then Mrs Stevenson, you know she is not a young woman, took ill and had to be taken home. And I think that Rosie has hardly left the hospital since then. But this morning she asked me to get in touch with you.'

'And Mrs Stevenson junior, what has become of her?' Sally asked.

'Oh, she has been taken into custody. She denies everything, of course, and it seems odd how all her nephews and nieces have disappeared. The boy Philip is with us now and he's glad to be here. The other girl, Lucy, well, she has gone to the elder daughter's, her married sister. The house is closed up and likely to remain so. Rosie is greatly upset because she is very fond of her father. And Miss Barrington, who, you know, instructs Rosie, has been a great help. She knows how to deal with reporters and such.'

It was at this point they realised that, Miss Collins having mentioned Miss Barrington and reporters, they were likely to be in for further long explanations. And then the front-door bell rang and Bill barked furiously. Fred got up to answer it and Sally said, 'I'm sorry, that was the dog barking, because we seem to have a visitor, but thank you very much indeed, Miss Collins, for ringing us to let us know what has happened. I'll be in touch with you again shortly. Give my best regards to Mrs Stevenson senior, please, will you?'

'I will, Mrs Carpenter, I will, and thank you. Goodbye.'

'Goodbye.'

Sally put down the phone and gasped, 'Oh, my goodness!'

She had never met Miss Collins but she had heard much about her. Everybody liked her, she was a good housekeeper and a friend to the old lady. Perhaps, though, what Miss Collins wasn't aware of herself was how much she was enjoying this event – it wasn't every day such sensational things happened in a family – and this had come over clearly in their telephone conversation. However, although Sally found Miss Collins's attitude slightly repellent, the events she had related went a long way to explain why the old lady would have nothing to do with her son's wife. She had obviously been right.

Fred now came in, saying, 'It was just a fellow collecting for the bazaar: had we any old clothes et cetera? How did you get rid of her?'

Sally looked at him as he sat down on the side of the couch. 'You felt the same as I did, then?'

'Yes. Yes. I've met so many Miss Collinses; they love giving you the gory details.'

She said nothing to this, but thought how often it was that they both came to the same opinion about a number of people . . . worthy people. Miss Collins, no doubt, could be classed as very worthy. Somehow, though, Sally didn't feel that Miss Barrington would fall within quite the same category.

'That woman must be a demon.'

'The mother?'

'Yes, of course the mother. And her husband was certainly very aware of it: look how he wasn't for letting Rosie out of his sight that day until he had her clear of the boat and her mother's hands. But to think that she would pay to have him polished off.'

Fred shook his head slowly as though he were unable to fathom the depths to which hate could sink. Not wanting to think about that, Sally said quickly, 'I'm going to phone the hospital and see if Rosie is there; she might be in the waiting room.'

'I would try her home first, but I'd wait an hour or so in case Miss Collins is hovering about.'

It was just after nine when Sally rang, and a young voice answered, saying, 'Yes? This is Mrs Stevenson's.'

'Oh, is that you, Philip? This is Mrs Carpenter here.'

'Oh; hello, Mrs Carpenter.' His voice was bright. 'You'll want to speak to Rosie?'

'Is she in?'

'She came in about ten minutes ago. I don't know whether she's in her bedroom or up in the schoolroom, but I'll get her for you.'

Sally waited a few minutes, and then a voice said, 'Oh, hello there. Am I glad to hear you!'

'Look, you've just got in, you must be very tired. I just want to know how your father is.'

'Dad's on the mend, thank God. And yes, I've just got in, and I am very tired; but I'd rather put off sleeping for another three days if I could have a word with you. I'm up in the school-room. I was getting a book to look at just in case I couldn't get to sleep. I haven't been to bed since Wednesday.'

'Oh, Rosie, you poor dear. It must have been awful for you. I wish we were nearer.'

'There's nobody wishes that more than me, I can tell you, Mr and Mrs C. Oh, yes, how I wish you both were nearer. Everybody's been so kind, and Miss Barrington has just gone home; she's been very good, seeing to things. And Miss Collins is up with Gran. I understand she gave you all the gen.'

'Yes. Yes, and more,' Sally replied, on a slight laugh.

'Have you ever noticed,' said Rosie, with a semblance of her old self, 'how good people can be boring?'

It was Fred now who got a word in first, saying, 'Rosie, you're telling me: there's no better bores than the good ones; but, then, they all mean well.'

'Yes; that's the awful thing about it,' said Rosie, 'they make you feel guilty. Anyway, dears, there's plenty of people, good and not so good, here that I could talk to, but I find that I can't open myself up somehow, except to Miss B; and then it's a different kind of talking. It's very strange, but there I was sitting by Dad last night in the hospital. It must have been about one o'clock this morning, really, and I was half dozing, thinking about you two and wondering why it was only a matter of a few weeks ago that I had first met you both. It seems as if I've known you for years and years and you were the only real people in my world. And, you know, when I did meet you the first time, it was with the boys; it was not until the second time, when I came back crying, that I really got to know you. I had always felt a great void inside. It seemed that people didn't really like me, in fact I knew my mother hated me, but I also felt there must be different people somewhere. There must be people who wouldn't look down their noses at me, there must be; but I never met them till I met you two, and you both jumped up from the couch and sat one on each side of me. You took my hands, and then you, Mrs C, took me into your arms, and somehow I knew that from that moment the void was filled; and no-one I have met since has added anything to it.'

'Oh, Rosie. Rosie. Here I go again. Even the thought of you makes me cry. We came into your life because you needed us, and you came into our lives because we needed you. We lost two babies a long time ago, we had neither a son nor a daughter. To us you're like a long-lost child, someone to help and love. Fred here saw that from the beginning, and also that there was amazing material in you; it just wanted bringing out. And he was right, but only up to a point, because I want something of the old Rosie to be still alive when the polished Rosie takes over.'

'Eeh, now!' Rosie's voice was cracking. 'I'm bubbling too. And I'll tell you it's very strange you saying that about remaining myself when the new Rosie takes over, because something like that came out the other afternoon between Miss Barrington and me. I was sitting exactly where I am now. It was the end of the session. It had been a long day and I knew I had done some good work and pleased her, for I'd made use of my first lessons in Latin and, feeling pretty satisfied with myself, I said, "Now that's put another layer on my façade." And what d'you think she said to that? In her stiffest of voices she said, "Rosie, all the façades in the world cannot blot out the real self underneath."

'When she said that, I came back with "Then there's little hope for me," to which her answer was, "It's up to you. It's only through time and will-power that you will find the answer. You have no control over your allotted span other than how you use it through the power of your will; and that, in the end, will prove that your façade, however thick you have made it, has not got rid of your real self. And if you are wise you won't allow it to: you will use your façade only as a means of taking you from one level to another and so behaving accordingly: not looking up your nose at some and down your nose at others. And if the façade is doing its work it will teach you to listen and not to show off to some bright spark that you know as much about a subject as he himself does. You will, I hope, come to learn that the clever people of this world, the really knowledgeable people like Socrates, will underplay themselves, and, like him, they, too, will speak the truth when they say that they're ignorant of so many things, that in fact they're still learning their own trade.

'"And you know," she went on, "I'm ignorant. Very ignorant. I'm known as a teacher of English, French and German. But also I like looking at paintings, yet what do I know about painting? I cannot put two colours together and produce a third; and I can hardly draw a straight line. Then there's music. I know what I like, but I can't play even one instrument. And politics too. I know little or nothing about politics, and the little I know I gather from the papers; and papers, as you know, glibly contradict each other, just as both sides in Parliament do, both declaring themselves right and never wrong. You never hear one side saying, 'Let us pause a moment and thrash this thing out together.' Well, that wouldn't be politics would it? As for science, I'm afraid even to think about science; and I have found out that very few people really know about science, but they think they are being very sharp when they ask questions, especially at intellectual meetings. Two sides may argue about God. Can one be a scientist and at the same time believe in God? That is a very common point, so often thrown around. Oh, my! *There's* a question that wants answering.

'"But I will tell you, Rosie, one thing I do believe in, and that is order. If you have order in a business, in a profession, in anything you take up, some good will come of it. As I see it, the order that keeps the cosmos in its various rotations is the same order that brightens a

231

home, gives success, as I've said, to a business or profession, which in itself gives purpose to life. I look up at the sky at night and I see it in motion, and its motion, as I discern it, spells order. So you could say, Rosie, there is one thing I do know besides teaching at various times English, Latin, French and German, and that is, I do know something about order. Which brings us back to you and your many façades. Well, wear as many as you like, my dear, but always remember that you cannot cover up yourself, not your real self."

'Then what d'you think she did, Mrs C? She patted my head, like you pat Bill's, and she walked out. But I didn't follow her. I took a pencil and I scribbled down practically word for word . . . well, not really exactly, but at least the gist of it as I've just told you.'

'Well, all I can say now,' said Fred, 'is I think you are a very clever girl, Rosie, and that memory of yours is going to take you places. At the same time, I think you have struck lucky with your tutor.'

And Sally now put in, 'And how do I see you, Rosie? I see you one day as the wife of a famous man, standing at the foot of a staircase receiving his guests, some' — she laughed now — 'with façades inches deep.'

It sounded as though Rosie was laughing and yet, at the same time, Sally wondered if she was crying as she spluttered, 'You know what I think? I think you are two of the nicest, kindest, loveliest and most highly polished liars in the world.'

'We mean it.' They said the words together; then Sally added, 'We do, Rosie, we do. We have felt from the beginning, and we have told you, you're going places. With your memory and determination there'll be nothing to stop you.'

'Unless she falls in love,' Fred put in, as an aside.

'Oh, no, Mr C; you needn't fear that. Not after what I've seen of marriage. You know, there are very few people like you two or Mr Watson and his funny little missus. You would think, for instance, that Peter was happily married, wouldn't you? Well, he's not. She's an out-and-out snob and she gives him a rough time, by what James says. By the way, James phoned here and told me all about your visit to the East End, at least your version of it, 'cos he stayed back with his mother. How he wishes he had been there. And don't you think it was wonderful of Charlie to do what he did for the Connollys? Even James knew nothing about this until Pontoon Mouth, as we called him, gave his father the paper bag to take to them, just before he flew back home, which, I suppose, is the last we'll see of him, anyway at this end.'

'Oh, no, it won't be,' Sally said, 'because you must have heard that he's going into business with his father, so he'll be back and forward here in the future.'

'Oh, yes, yes. But have you ever heard, Mrs C, of a heavy whisky drinker going on the wagon? He might for a week or two but he'll slide back. There was a place near us in Birmingham where they paid the earth to be dried out; at least, somebody paid the earth to have it done; but they started soaking again once they got through those gates. Anyway, time will tell. But it was nice of him, I must admit, to get the Connollys out of what James said was a stinking hole. They were such a good family and they fell in with the scheme and carried it out right to the end, particularly the girl called Mattie.'

There was the sound of a door opening and a voice calling, and Rosie answered, 'All right,

Phil; tell Gran I'm going to bed this minute.'

'She'll send Miss Collins up, and she'll put you to bed.'

'I don't think I want that, do you?' said Rosie *sotto voce*. 'Anyway, I'm standing here with my eyes closed.'

'Well, get yourself off!' said Fred, sharply. 'There'll be plenty of time for talking later.'

'Good night, Rosie,' Sally said softly. 'Ring again soon; I want to hear more about Miss Barrington.'

'I will, Mama. I will, Papa.' Then on a laugh, she added, 'Good night, love. Pat Bill for me.'

8

Rosie telephoned the carpenters two or three times before the trial of her mother and the men she had paid to murder her husband. Her father was now at home and being nursed and pampered by his mother; and he was so glad, they could gather from what she said, that he had the boy with him, and of course Rosie herself. Although she didn't put it into words they could see that her father was claiming a lot of her attention.

When the day of the trial came, the two men escaped the charge of attempted murder because no implement that could have inflicted the wound at the back of Mr Stevenson's head had been found on them, or anything on the ground about except a lump of sharp rock near where he was lying.

The two men charged had been very open

about the whole thing, and in doing so had exposed the power their aunt held over her family. Of course they couldn't prove that they hadn't set out to murder him, they could only keep repeating that before they attacked him they had told themselves that they weren't going to do him in and that whatever happened they were going to inform the police anonymously over the phone afterwards that a man needing attention was lying at a certain place.

Asked why they ran from the scene, they said that their victim had been handing out punishment too, as could be seen from their own faces; but they became frightened when he fell to the ground and then didn't move. Anyway, the charge had been for assault and battery and for co-operating with the prisoner to do her husband harm. Their plea was that they knew she wanted him murdered but they weren't going to carry that out, although she had paid them at least part of the sum promised if he were found dead.

All through the case Florence Stevenson swore that the men had made this up because she had refused to loan them money, and she also insisted that she had no ill will against her husband. At one stage she was asked by the prosecuting counsel why, then, when the police came to arrest her, was she ready for flight? Her two suitcases were not only packed with clothes but with a large number of bank notes. As for her big handbag, that too was full of paper money, together with three well-stocked building society booklets.

She was found guilty of inciting to murder and was jailed for ten years. Her two frightened nephews were given five years each.

Yet poor Mr Stevenson was not yet finished with trouble. On that particular Saturday morning after leaving the boat with Rosie, he had gone straight to his solicitor and started divorce proceedings; and the outcome of the murder case against his wife had helped to shorten the time for the divorce to be made absolute. But during this period of waiting while he convalesced with his mother, leaving the factory in the capable hands of Mr Jackson and his departmental heads, he corresponded with his former mistress, who now suggested that she move to be nearer him. He immediately telephoned her and told her not to do this. He had been thinking the matter over, he said, and she would not find him ungenerous, she would not want for anything; he would see to that. The telephone went down with a bang and within twenty-four hours she appeared on the doorstep of his mother's house and demanded to see him. When told he was in the office she said she would wait until he returned.

His mother, Mrs Stevenson, had never met her son's mistress, and what she saw of her now caused her both surprise and dislike. The surprise was that she was quite a youngish woman in her early forties, and she was obviously well educated. Definitely she was a woman with her wits about her, and both Miss Collins and Miss Barrington found that here was a woman who wasn't to be pushed or talked off. So George Stevenson on his return was made aware of his visitor before he entered the morning room.

Rosie said that her dad's voice had been quiet when he greeted her with, 'Hello, Iris. I'm surprised to see you.' She had answered him to the effect that he shouldn't be, as she had looked after him for nine years and at one time he had talked of marrying her. Rosie said that although his voice did not rise, he strongly reminded her that more recently he had warned her that if he were ever free he would never marry again. 'Now I *am* free,' he said, 'I'm not going to marry

239

you or anyone else. So there you have it.'

To this she had answered, 'Well, there's a way to make you change your mind. I'm going on a fortnight's holiday. I wouldn't go now only it is already booked, but when I come back I hope you will be seeing things in a different light. Don't forget, George, that I have lived with you and mothered you and listened to your moans about your wife and family for nine years. I was a young woman when you bought that house, and then all you wanted was to live with me for ever, for you were sick of the tribe your wife had about you. You were a man twenty-odd years my senior, to me an old man, but you talked me into it and you got the house and I made it a home for you.'

'Aye, and everything had to be the best, hadn't it? And your housekeeping money would've kept a family of ten going. I wasn't stupid or blind.'

'Well, George, I advise you not to go on being stupid or blind, that's if you know what's good for you, because I might be tempted to take you to court.'

'The minute she was out of the door,' Rosie said, 'Dad was on the phone to his solicitor and put the situation before him, and the solicitor said that he should immediately have a board put up outside to say that the house was for sale, together with its contents.

'Well, the board wasn't up a matter of days, before it was down. One of the single men who had come south when the factory moved to London was getting married and wanted to start up a home for his wife. This house seemed to be the very thing. So that part was ended. Another was that Dad had left with his solicitor a letter saying that he would pass over to Iris a considerable sum of money if she refrained from any legal process.'

Apparently that was the end of George Stevenson's plight as far as the Carpenters were concerned, for they heard no more of the matter from Rosie and concluded that the offered settlement had proved too hard for Iris to resist.

After all the excitement, life seemed to settle down. Soon Fred and Sally had resumed their quiet existence of work and domesticity.

As the austerity of the post-war years gradually relaxed, holidays abroad were becoming a possibility, and new ideas and fabrics were available for doing up their house, so that they felt it was becoming more their own and had begun to throw off the sadness of the past.

And trade was beginning to improve too. Sally had made several trips to London to investigate the fashion scene, and now ordered regularly from a number of manufacturers with whom she had established contact there. Her shop, Eve, was considered fashionable locally, and Sally was finding a year-by-year increase in her turnover, and in her profits. Greatly daring, she had taken on extra help – a pleasant, enthusiastic school leaver from the girls' grammar school called Janice. Once she had trained the girl, who turned out to have excellent dress sense, Sally felt she could go away occasionally. Then the wife of a colleague of Fred's, who was at a loose end because her family had grown up and left home, was glad to help Janice in the shop.

News of Rosie came at more irregular intervals now. First she was working hard with Miss Barrington and then had moved on to Miss Clarke's school, St Chide's. During the next three years she only came for the weekend once.

Rosie then was just on eighteen years old, and to the onlooker there was now certainly no semblance of Rosie of the River. She was tall, five foot seven and a half. She was slim. She had beautiful dark wavy hair. She had a creamy skin, a pair of laughing eyes, and a large well-shaped mouth, and she carried herself like a duchess.

She had stayed a full year with Miss Barrington, and had toured France with her, when she sent them postcards giving her impression of different places, in particular her annoyance at Notre Dame where she had to pay sixpence to get into a room to see the bejewelled vestments of popes and bishops, and gold chalices and salvers, while outside, on the steps, sat the poor and hungry begging for money. Nor was she impressed with Versailles, all those rooms glorified by wealth. No wonder there had been a number of revolutions in the country. She wasn't, in fact, all that taken with the French although she spoke their language well.

On her visit she was delighted with their home, and didn't bother that it felt like an icebox after her granny's large, centrally heated house. What they recalled afterwards of that weekend was how the three of them talked and laughed and became closer still. On leaving, Sally begged her to make visits more often. She did them so much good and she seemed to love them both – and Bill, of course. Oh, yes, Bill.

Sally asked her if it was accidental or on

purpose that Miss Barrington had always seemed to make it impossible for her to spend another weekend away from home: they were to tour Germany or Spain, or they were to meet this important person or that one.

Rosie had laughed at this, but nevertheless did not say they were wrong, only that Briggy seemed to know a lot of very influential people who, incidentally, had got her into the Diplomatic Service when she left school in a year's time, and how could they expect her to answer that question when she was a budding diplomat?

This had set them off into a gale of laughter; she had become once again the girl they remembered, relating a recent event which might have had dire repercussions on her career. And here the Carpenters had to admit to themselves that thankfully Miss Barrington's presence and influence had smoothed things over.

Rosie had been two years at St Chide's when the incident happened. Her first year at the school had shown surprising results, all due to Miss Barrington, of course. She had been given an A for her English and a B for Latin, an A for French, a B for German and Bs for history and geography. But she was right at the bottom in painting, drawing and music. However, in spite of this, her progress was sufficient to make her into one of the school's flyers. In her second year she had got As in English, Latin, French and German and Bs in History, Maths and Science.

She had written to the Carpenters the day the results were made public, saying it had all been wonderful; the whole family were there to celebrate, she said, the only two missing were Mr and Mrs C.

It was about two months later, at the beginning of an additional third year, that Miss Rosina Stevenson blotted her copybook. And how they laughed as she told them about it, although it might have meant the end of any hopes of a career.

It concerned one Constance Victoria Fordstone-Grey, the last names being hyphenated. On this particular day she was among a clique of girls from her dormitory, five in all, when in Rosie's hearing, she said, 'They used only to allow decent families here in this school. Things are changing. You used to have to be out of the top drawer.'

Apparently, Rosie had turned to one of the two friends who were walking with her, and said in no small voice, 'It's amazing the reproductions that are on the market today. In the old days anything known as coming out of the top drawer was given one single name, such as a chest or a commode, but now the reproductions, in order to give them some foundation, hyphenate their names. Old English names, especially those in the top drawers, were, as I said, simple names. Of course, the real people know when it's a reproduction once the fakes open their mouths.'

'Well,' cried Miss Constance Victoria Fordstone-Grey, 'you have done that already, haven't you?'

'Me?' responded Rosie innocently, looking at the other girl, who was almost a head taller than her, with thick brown hair and very muscular legs, squarely in the eye. 'But I am not out of the top drawer, I'm a very ordinary individual. The only thing is, I happen to be more clever than some people, but just in different ways.'

'Of course you're more clever, the daughter of a woman who tried to murder her husband and is now doing ten years in jail for it. And you wouldn't have been here if it hadn't been for your father, who is a dirty old man who kept a mistress on the side. Your ancestry was certainly an open book in the papers – reproduction top drawer as may be, but you're from the gutter, from where Miss Barrington dragged you up and taught you. But for her you would not be here today, because you could not speak even one word of correct English. She hammered it into you for a year, but even so she was unable to hide the slut in you, because that's all you are, a guttersnipe slut.'

Gone was the façade. It was as if the wind had whipped Rosie naked, for she simply leaped at her tormentor and brought her hand with a crashing slap across the side of her tall opponent's face. But when her hair was grabbed in both hands and as she felt it being torn from her head she let out a scream; then bringing her knee up, well under her opponent's short hockey skirt, she caused that young lady's hands to loosen from her hair and grip her stomach. Then Miss Fordstone-Grey found herself gripped by the collar of her sports shirt and being swung round. When the toe of Miss Rosina Stevenson's hockey boot seemed to embed itself in her nether quarters, she leaped clumsily into a shallow ditch bordering the playing field.

The commotion had brought teachers and pupils from other parts of the field, and one of the teachers was demanding an explanation.

'You *what*?' she shouted at Rosie, who answered quite plainly for everyone to hear: 'I kicked her in the arse, and I've been wanting to do that for some time because I'm sick and tired of her innuendoes and insults. I'm not putting up with it any more from her or from anyone else.' The result was that she was immediately ordered to make herself ready for a visit to the Headmistress.

As she said to Fred and Sally, she felt it was to be the end of her days there, but she wasn't sorry: she knew she was capable of going out into the world now and finding a job. Yet she also knew she wasn't quite ready: she wanted to get more languages into her head, as many as were needed to be an interpreter. An interpreter she meant to be, and Miss Barrington, too, acknowledged she was indeed cut out to be one.

Poor Rosie, the Carpenters thought. But they still laughed at the thought of her kicking the so-called lady in the hindquarters and not moderating her explanation to the teacher. There must have been an uproar in the school that day!

When later, she was called before the head and her deputy, also seated in the office were the

French teacher, the history teacher and the games instructor.

Rosie of the River was still very much to the fore as she stood in front of these five ladies and was asked to explain the meaning of her behaviour towards another pupil, and at least Miss Clarke herself was not surprised at the simple and straightforward reply: 'I'd stood enough,' Rosie had said. 'I never passed her or her cronies without some jibe being thrown at me, though I never replied for I remembered my first training under Miss Barrington. She would have said, "Just that will puzzle them more than anything." It has been difficult advice to take, but I've taken it up till today.'

'And what caused you to change your attitude today?' demanded Miss Clarke.

'Because she said that the policy of this school had changed. At one time only those out of the top drawer were taken in. That was too much of a quip for me to resist, and I replied that it was a pity they were making so many reproductions now, or words to that effect.'

'I swear Miss Clarke gave a sort of hiccup and cough to hide a spurt of laughter. So I went on and told them exactly what Miss Constance

Victoria Fordstone-Grey said about my parents, and about Miss Barrington having, as she said, to drag me from the gutter; that she even had to teach me how to speak in English before I was allowed here.'

Apparently, here Rosie had choked before she could add, 'She said that no wonder my mother was a murderess and doing ten years because she tried to kill her husband as he, a dirty old man, had been living with a mistress, and it all had been headlines. I – I couldn't stand that. Now could I? It was too much, and so I let blaze . . . You all know the rest.'

'After much more palaver,' she continued, 'Miss Clarke broke in, saying stiffly now, "We've heard enough. Go to your room, Rosina. We shall call you later."'

And it wasn't until some time later, in fact the following day, that Rosie knew that her two friends and the five friends of the injured person so-called were summoned to appear before the same committee of ladies. Rosie's two friends gave their version of what had transpired word for word, only adding that they were surprised that Rosie had done what she did because she had put up with Miss Constance Victoria Fordstone-Grey's taunting for a long time. Two of the other five girls had quite a different version. It was said that Rosina Stevenson would always aggravate a situation with her quips. The other three girls, however, admitted that it wasn't until Constance had spoken of Rosie's mother being a murderess and her father a dirty old man that Rosina retaliated angrily.

After the girls were dismissed it would appear that the French mistress was in favour of overlooking the whole thing, as was the deputy head, but the games mistress was for Rosina being expelled, and added that the art mistress and the music mistress and others, if asked their opinion, would agree with her. To this Miss Clarke had replied that she wasn't asking for the opinions of other teachers.

It was twelve hours later, after a conference between Miss Barrington and Miss Clarke, that Rosie was called into the Head's office again.

The Head was alone now. She did not tell Rosie to sit down but she spoke to her plainly, as Rosie herself would have spoken, and she said, 'The decision is that you may stay on at this school. I have known from the first that you are highly intelligent and that you might make an excellent scholar. I also know that a leopard never changes its spots; and here the only thing we hope to do is to cover them over. The same expression you yourself once used to me: it was hiding oneself under a façade. You have done this, and I will say very well too; but now it's up to you whether you are to finish here or not. In any case, you will now be moved into a different dormitory, of three only. It will come under the care of Miss Weir.'

Rosie was highly relieved that the outcome was no worse than this. Miss Weir, she already knew, was a very strict disciplinarian. When she said lights out, no repeat order was ever required. And this, Rosie ruefully admitted to herself, could only be to her benefit in her final year at the school.

9

It must have been towards the end of the fifties when Fred and Sally were in the wood one day trying to prise up the roots of an old willow tree. With the increasing success of Eve, they had been able finally to give up the unequal struggle to go on trying to live in Aunt Grace's house in comfort, and had sold it to a couple from Basingstoke who wanted to turn it into a guesthouse. Their new home, Fairmile, was close by, on a road leading up to a wood. It was a charming house, but it only had a small garden, so piece by piece, when they could afford it, they had bought part of the wood that adjoined it. It was overgrown with old trees and stumps of others cut down for firewood during the war and would take several years to create the garden they dreamed of, but here they were, making a start.

Fred had dug deep all round the old roots and cut through them, leaving the main stump for Sally to bend back and forward in an attempt to loosen it. Twice, thinking they heard a call, they stopped. The third time, they looked at each other, then Fred jumped out of the hole and followed his wife to the edge of the wood and within sight of the house. There stood a young lady, calling, 'Where are my papa and mama?'

They both shouted, 'Rosie! Rosie!' Then the three of them were enfolded in each other's arms. 'Why didn't you let us know?' Sally cried. 'Just look at us!'

'Yes, I am; I'm looking at you, and you're wonderful.' Rosie kissed her for the second or third time. 'And look at my dear papa; he's in a mess. Why must you work like this?'

'Why don't you shut up and let us get inside?' answered Fred, with a grin from ear to ear.

An hour later they were sitting round the fire in the drawing room and she was exclaiming yet again what a lovely house this was, quite different from the old one, so beautifully built and proportioned. They had to confess that they still hadn't got around to installing central heating, any more than they had at the previous house, but they had an Aga in the kitchen, and that was wonderful. And so it went on all during tea, and long after.

Rosie told them about the loss of her granny, and about her father gradually letting go of work and handing everything over to Philip, who was a marvellous manager. 'And what d'you think?' she put in at one point, 'He, I mean Philip, goes to Miss Barrington for language lessons. He's studying both French and German. He wants to go over to Europe and see for himself how trade goes on in his business there and to make contacts. He certainly has a business head on his shoulders, has Phil, but fancy him going to old Briggy for language lessons, just as I did. But from what she tells me I'm afraid he finds it a little more difficult. I've been lucky, she's always reminding me, lucky with having a good memory. And guess where I'm going next?'

'Germany?' said Fred.

'No. Belgium, Brussels, the embassy there. I'm to be a first assistant and interpreter to—' She now stopped and slapped her own cheek, saying, 'Remember what you're told, woman: no names! So all I'm going to say to you, dear Papa, is I've been employed as interpreter to a certain gentleman of high standing, and I was the chosen one of nine.' Then turning back to Sally, she said, in her old voice, 'You could've knocked me down with a sledge-hammer. You could, Mrs C, you could. I felt, although it would be promotion, it would be a cushy job. But it'll be no cushy job, for it really is a big step forward. I shall meet some of the mighty of the day. Oh, you wouldn't believe it! Yes, I have already met quite a few people like that, but from a back seat as it were. Now I'm in the front stalls and this is where I wanted to be. The next place will be the stage.'

'There's nothing wrong with an opinion of yourself, is there, Miss Rosie of the River?'

'No, sir; not a thing wrong about that. I knew where I was going, at least have known where I wanted to go, from the beginning. I thought I'd been educated at that school. You're never educated until you get out into the world and you meet these people, these so-called high-ups. Oh, how glad I am that Rosie Stevenson is still underneath: I can pick them out while they are smiling and shaking hands and bowing. Oh, yes, there are lots of people you have to bow to, and occasionally a few you've got to curtsy to. Would you believe that, Mrs C?'

'Anything you say I'll believe, Rosie,

anything. Oh, and you look marvellous, wonderful. You look so . . . well . . . like . . . what can I say?'

'An upstart?'

'No, never that.' Fred was shaking his head, and his wife with him.

Then Sally said, 'The only way I can put it, you look like some distinguished gentleman's lady wife. I can see you standing at the foot of the stairs receiving the guests.'

'Oh, Mrs C!' Rosie started to laugh and it was a cracked laugh. 'You won't believe this, but I had to stand in for someone who had been taken ill, and that's exactly what I had to do, stand at the foot of the stairs and welcome the guests. I got a new dress specially.'

They all laughed now, but stopped when, looking at Fred, she said, 'It's funny, Mr C, but in jobs like these I have found that men are afraid of each other. Women aren't so much, no. But what am I thinking about? They're mostly being kept by the men who, probably, they keep pushing from behind. Oh, yes, they do; in many cases it's evident. And you know' – she looked from one to the other of them – 'at times I'm glad I was brought up as I was because then, being pushed aside as if I were nothing, I had time to look at people, to study them, and it helps me now.

'Anyway, enough about me. What about you, Mrs C? You're looking very elegant these days.'

Sally felt that in comparison to the glittering world which from now on would be the back-cloth to Rosie's life, her own success with Eve was a modest affair. Nevertheless, she was proud of it, and was able to make Rosie laugh with her stories about some of the mishaps that had befallen her on her early buying trips to London, and her comments on the fashion world which she now felt herself to be a part of.

'There's another thing, or person, we've never spoken about,' said Rosie, after a pause in the conversation. 'I know, because I keep putting my hand out and wanting to stroke his head. He must have been a great loss.'

Fred and Sally looked at each other; then they both smiled at her. 'We can talk about him now, dear,' Sally said. 'We couldn't at one time; he was like our first child. We mourn him more than we shall any relative who is likely to die.'

'Are you thinking about getting another?' Rosie asked quietly.

'Yes; we are thinking about having a labrador. But it's not going to be easy.'

Being a sensitive creature, Rosie must have noticed the sadness that had come upon them both for she suddenly turned about and beat the back of the sofa as she cried, 'Fancy me forgetting to tell you this bit of news!'

'What bit of news?' said Fred, now interested.

'Who d'you think I saw just this last week?'

'Well, we'll never know unless you tell us; we don't move in your world, do we?' Sally said.

'Do you remember Pontoon Mouth?'

'Remember Pontoon Mouth? Of course we remember Pontoon Mouth, or Whalemouth as you called him. What's happened to him?'

'Oh, what hasn't happened to him? Did you know he got married?'

'No, we didn't. Where d'you get all your news from?' Fred asked.

'Oh, from Watson, Wheeler and Co. It's run mostly by James, I might tell you, and he's up to his eyes since his poor old father died. That was a shame, because he was a wonderful man.'

'Yes, he was,' Sally put in. 'He was marvellous. But go on, tell us more about Whalemouth.'

'Well, he got married, but it lasted only nine months.'

'She was sick of his mouth by then, I suppose,' said Fred. 'Although I must admit there was another side to him, which I recognised after the Connolly episode on that particular Saturday afternoon.'

'Is he back on the booze?' Sally asked.

'I wouldn't really know,' said Rosie. 'Yet I met him at a do when I saw him with a glass in his hand, and then I realised that he was drinking lime and soda.'

'Did you have a talk with him?' asked Fred.

'Well, a short one. He came straight at me, crying, "Rosie! Rosie Stevenson, as ever was!" I nearly turned on him and said, "Whalemouth! As ever was," but remembering my tutors, I said simply, "My! What are you doing here? How's America getting on without you?"

'"Very well, I understand," he said; "that's until I return, which will be next week."

'"Is your family over there?" I asked.

'"Family?" He raised his thick eyebrows at me and said, "I haven't any family, Rosie."

'"But I understood you were married."

'"I was for nine long months." He shook his head slowly back and forward and repeated, "Nine long months . . ."

'"And then you divorced her?"

'"No, Rosie; she divorced me."

'"Well, you must've been very wicked."

'"Yes, I was very wicked. I enjoy being wicked, Rosie, as you must remember."

'"Well, all I can say is I hope she made you pay for your pleasure."

'"She did indeed. She only wanted ten million dollars. Anyway we settled for five."

'"And that's what you gave her, five million?" I said, looking at him quite seriously. "You gave her only five million?"

'"Yes, that's all, Rosie, five million."

'I couldn't help it, but Rosie of the River came back and I said, "You are a mean bugger, aren't you?"'

Sally and Fred were now lying against each other on the couch, shaking with laughter, and Rosie, laughing too, spluttered, 'He put his head back and cried, "And there was I, making another mistake, thinking you had been trained to be a lady. James had also told me you were a first-class interpreter." Then his voice changed and he said, "Rosie, let's have dinner together," and I pulled away from him and said, "D'you want to tie my shoelaces again?" Now we were drawing attention to our corner of the room and I said quite seriously, "Please! Please, do not make me laugh or come out with such vulgarities; I have a very special job to live up to." Again he said, softly, "Do have dinner with me. What about tomorrow at the Ritz, eh? What about it?"

' "I can't. I'm sorry, Charles, I'm off to Holland tomorrow."

' "Holland?" he said. "What are you doing there?"

' "I don't know," I said. "I've only been told I have to go to Holland. I'm an interpreter, you know, I don't make the decisions."

' "Yes. Yes; I know," and then laughing gently he said, "I wonder what you would come out with if during one of those sessions you spoke your thoughts aloud?"

' "I wonder, too, Charles."

' "How long do you expect to be in Holland?"

' "I haven't any idea," I said.

' "Well, Rosie, I'd like us to have a bit of a natter again some time. How can I look you up?"

' "You can't, sir. You can't."

' "Haven't you a phone number?"

' "No, only when I was at home."

' "What is that?"

' "I'm sorry; I don't give my phone number to strange men."

' "Don't be silly. I can always ask James."

' "Well, I can always tell James not to give it to you."

' "Well," he said now, "he's a parson, so I'll let him decide. You know something?" He stepped back from me. "No-one would believe that the little firebrand who has a punch like a middleweight and a knee like a wrestler's, not to speak of a foot that she puts in places that she shouldn't, could turn into such a beautiful piece of humanity and look so beguiling that one would think butter wouldn't melt in her mouth."

'I laughed outright saying, "All right; we'll have lunch some day. That's a promise."

' "But when?"

' "When I'm back in England and when you're over from America."

'He now leaned towards me and in the politest of voices he said, "You know what you are, Rosie Stevenson? You're a tantalising little bitch. No, not a little one, a tall, elegant one. But wait, I'll see my day with you; I never break a promise I make to myself." He moved aside, saying, "Oh dear! There's someone waiting anxiously for me to tell them more lies." And I, too, looked sideways, and saw three gentlemen standing looking towards us; so we nodded to each other and went on our ways.'

'Poor Charlie.'

She was shaking her head at Fred, 'Poor Charlie indeed! What's poor about him? He blows his nose on five-pound notes.'

'Rosie! Rosie!'

'Yes, Mama. Yes, Mama. I know; she's still there, the common slut. Poor Miss Barrington, she's wasted her time, hasn't she? So did Miss Clarke and the rest of them.'

'Nobody ever wasted their time on you, Rosie,' said Fred; 'I said one day you'd get there, didn't I? That you'd go places? I can see you married to one of the big noises. Oh, yes, I can. Can't you, dear?'

Sally looked at him, thought for a moment, and then said, 'I don't just want to see her married, Fred, to one of the big noises; I want to see her married to someone she loves and that she'll settle down with, and make a home for them and have children.' As if Rosie weren't there, she continued, 'She wants to marry someone who needs her.'

'What are you talking about, Mrs C, someone that needs me? *I* need somebody. *I* need a shoulder to cry on. I haven't had one since I cried on yours, and that's a fact.' She now looked towards Fred, then back to Sally. 'I once said to you that the void in me wasn't filled till that day I lay on your shoulder in the boat and cried. I go home and there is Father who needs me and says why don't I settle down and stay at home; there's Miss Collins who needs someone to unburden herself to; even our Phil needs me. He's shy with girls. And when he says he's looking for one like me, I say God help him. It's me who needs someone, and I found someone that day on the boat.'

She put out a hand and stroked Sally's face. There were tears in her eyes as she went on, 'But I'm in all corners of the world when suddenly I need you, because, you know, I'm not just a clever clogs with a good memory, I'm Rosie Stevenson who wants a mother, a sister, a friend, and in that moment in that boat you became all those things to me, and so did Fred.'

She put out a hand towards him, and he gripped it and said, 'You say you need us. Well, like the rest of them at your home, we need you. We need to know that you're there, somewhere in the world bringing brightness into somebody's life, because you know, Rosie, you have this power; whether you're swearing and cursing or not you still have this ability. It's a wonderful thing to have, people needing you. Just think of it that way.'

And now Sally put in, 'That's it. That's it: think of it that way until you meet somebody that you need in a different way altogether, and he'll come along, you'll see.'

Jerking himself along the couch, Fred said shakily, 'How the hell is it that whenever we three get together we cry? We're up the pole, the three of us. Forget now about the men in the future, tell us about the men in your past. One thing I want to know, have you been proposed to?'

Rosie was laughing now. 'Yes, twice, and seriously.'

'What were they?' Sally asked. 'I mean, what did they do?'

'You're another one who wants me to marry money.'

'Yes, of course, to keep you in the way you should be kept. Go on, tell me what they were.'

'Well, the first one was nearly old enough to be my father. He was fourteen years my senior, but he was nice. He was charming and he was persistent. But the only thing I don't want to be in this world is a stepmother, and his wife had died, leaving him with a son of four years old and a girl of six, and although I liked him very much, yes, indeed I did – his position was important enough to satisfy even you, and he had not only a town house but a country house and well – I ask you both, can you see me being a stepmother?'

After some thought, Sally said, 'No, perhaps not; but it's a pity because he sounds nice.'

'He was nice. He still is nice, and he still keeps asking me.'

'What about the other one?' said Fred.

'Oh, there was a different kettle of fish! He was only two years older than me, the youngest son of a county family. There were five brothers, no girls at all. He was in the Diplomatic Service; a bit like myself, he had gone in for languages. We went out to dinner and then saw quite a lot of each other, when he talked much about his family. They lived in an old manor house. Only two of the other brothers were married; his father who used to deal with stocks and shares or something like that, was eaten up with arthritis and so was bound to a wheelchair; his mother was a very busy woman. He'd like to take me down there as his prospective wife, he said, to meet her and the rest of them. However, I didn't go down there to meet her and the rest of them, because I found he was much more interested in my father's factory than in me; and when he eventually found out the factory would be left to my brother – I had told Dad I never wanted anything to do with it – he definitely cooled off towards me. But, of course, there is still the widower hanging on, and I have promised to give him my answer when he returns from abroad next year.'

With all their talk and revived memories, it had been a wonderful weekend. Sally and Fred were not to know that it would be nearly another ten years before they'd all meet up again, and that many things were to take place before that, not only in Rosie's life but in their own.

10

Rosie's work meant that she was endlessly travelling and was more often outside the country than at home. When she telephoned it was often from remote cities, and when she was on leave there somehow seemed very little time to get down to visit them. She said nothing more about the widower, and Sally quietly noted that she had obviously decided against marriage to him.

Sally herself was increasingly busy. When her assistant, Janice, married and moved to Brighton in the early sixties, Sally had offered to open a new branch of Eve there that would cater for the tastes of the younger generation if Janice would manage it. This had turned out to be such a success that two more shops were opened, in Eastbourne and Canterbury, and now the size of Sally's orders to the dress manufacturers was such that she had become a valuable customer, whose opinions they listened to. She left the ordering of the younger styles to Janice after she made her a partner in 1965, but still ordered for a slightly older market herself for all the shops. As she said to Fred, in her thirties and forties she had spent many hours searching for stylish and pretty clothes that were suitable for her own age group, and she still had a good eye for what she could sell in an increasingly prosperous market.

The years of hard work came to an end in 1967, when a retailing group based in London that was looking to expand its fashion side made her an offer that she, Janice and Fred decided they couldn't refuse. The Carpenters were now able to contemplate a comfortable retirement free of worry, and Fred gave up work too.

It was at this point that a telephone call came from Rosie.

'I rang to congratulate you, Mama and Papa, but mostly Mama, on this splendid sale. I just cannot get over it that you did it all on your own, you clever woman.'

'Well, it's certainly nice to feel that all our financial worries about the future are at an end. We still can't really believe it's true, and we have to keep reminding ourselves that it is. When you can get down here what we want to do is celebrate it properly, just the three of us.'

'Don't worry, I will, I certainly will, though it may take a little time to organise that, but I'll be in touch just as soon as I can.'

'We know how busy you are, but we'll really look forward to it. What's the news at your end?'

'You'll never guess what happened yesterday. I ran into Charlie again, you know, Whalemouth.'

'Yes; yes,' Sally said. 'I know. And did you go out to dinner with him?'

'No, I didn't, although he persisted. He's been married again.'

'Never!'

'Yes, he has, and divorced.'

'No!' Sally laughed. 'Not again!'

'Yes. This one lasted only three months.'

'Surely not? She couldn't divorce him, or he couldn't divorce her in three months.'

'My! You don't know what goes on in America. She did, dear. Yes, she did. But this time she got only three million dollars out of him. "Poor sod!" I said. "That's all you gave her?"'

Sally had always winced when someone used

271

the word 'sod', but when Rosie said it she burst out laughing and repeated, 'And she only got three million?'

'Yes; I called him a mean scrub. Three solid months of her life and only three million dollars for it.'

It was some two years later that Fred and Sally received a long letter from Rosie. She was in France, where she'd had another proposal of marriage, which she had refused. But she said she realised she was thirty-five now, and she wanted children.

However, there was a sequel to the story of Whalemouth, though it was not to come for another six months, when one night Rosie phoned, as she often did at weekends.

'What I'm going to do is to come down to you on Friday night and ask if you can put me and my friend up for the weekend.'

'Of course. Of course, my dear. Bring as many friends as you like.'

'I have only one and we shall appear on Friday evening about six o'clock. All right?'

'All right, my dear. Yes, of course, all right.'

'Bye-bye, Mama. Give my love to Papa.'

'Bye-bye, you little devil,' Sally said, and put the phone down.

Within another hour, they received a call from James Watson, asking if they had heard from Rosie and if she had given them her news. When they said no, he replied, 'Good! I can tell you that I'm very happy.' That's all he would say. She had said there was another man in her life and she must have found love. Apparently the man was James.

Why were they both disappointed? It was Sally who voiced it, saying, 'She's throwing her life away, living down in the East End with her talents. All right, she might love him, who wouldn't?, but if only he'd move to a different parish and give himself a break. She'll need a break, too, working down there after the life she's led for so long. Do you know? She's been in practically every quarter of the globe, except perhaps the very Far East. She's lived among very clever and important people, and she's been treated like someone with a brain. She looks like a model but she has a brain. No wonder James is happy.'

'You always said it didn't matter about position or anything else so long as she was happy.

Now you have to let her see that you were right. Let them both see that you were right,' said Fred mildly.

'Yes, I know,' Sally said. 'Yes, I said that. But somehow I saw her living in a nice house and going places. I wonder what her father will think. It's a good job her granny's dead for I don't think she'd welcome a parson into the family, not in this way anyhow, not for her Rosie. I can't help it' – she stood up – 'I think she's going to waste her life.'

'Now, look here! You'll have to get out of that mood before they come. And it will likely be in that old bone-shaker of his. We've also got to get that drain cleared, at least part of the way, because it's so full of soil now that if it rains it'll pour over and down the drive and into the kitchen. Not to say that his old bone-shaker won't slide down the drive with it.'

They lived on a private road and had to keep clear the two-feet-deep ditch that ran alongside it. It passed the three large houses above them further up the road. When they didn't bother about the ditches the rain poured down the middle of the road until it came to the Carpenters' drain, which it filled, and if the houses below them didn't clear their part of the ditch the water just flowed over in front of their gates and down their very winding drive that led straight into the kitchen. It was navvies' work clearing that ditch, but all the work they did outside seemed to be navvies' work and Fred would not have help.

So there they were, on the Friday morning, Fred shovelling the grit and dirt out of the ditch and Sally putting it in the barrow and wheeling it away.

Few cars used the road, but one was now coming in sight. It was a very large one and Fred said, 'If he drives too near the edge of the ditch and pushes this mess back into it I'll pull him out and rub his nose in it.'

The big car continued slowly on. It caused them to straighten their backs and look at it. Fred said, under his breath, 'It's a Daimler. I wonder where that's for?'

The car stopped a few yards before their own gate, which was very like a field gate. As far as they could see there were two people in it. The far door opened and a man got out. He was very tall, broad, and smiling. He went round to the other side and out stepped a lady, and they both stood on the path and looked towards the two labourers who were staring at them, before they both cried together, 'Rosie! Rosie!' Then they were running towards their visitors, only to stop dead and for Fred to put his hands up, filthy with mud, and cry, 'Don't come a step nearer. Not now! Not now! My God, the condition we're in! You weren't supposed to be here till late this afternoon.'

'Where's . . . ?' Sally just stopped herself from saying James as she looked at the tall man. He looked at her, and putting out his hand, he grabbed her dirty one, saying, 'Hello, Mrs C.'

She nearly said, 'Whalemouth!' Instead she stammered, 'You're . . . you're Charlie.'

'Yes, ma'am, indeed I'm Charlie. And you've heard a lot about me, right from the time my wife put her foot in my backside.'

'Your . . . ?' But Rosie was upon Sally now, her arms around her neck.

Fred said, 'For God's sake! Let's get out of this and indoors and cleaned up. Well, I'll be damned!'

Charlie was now shaking Fred's muddy hand and Fred was saying, 'So you're Charlie!' followed yet again by, 'Well, I'll be damned!'

'Well, let's all be damned but let's get inside. I'm frozen,' Sally said.

It was half an hour later when Fred and she

were cleaned up and he had made coffee and they were all sitting in the drawing room, the Carpenters to one side of the fire, Rosie and the handsome brown-haired man on the other, sitting very close on the sofa.

Fred was saying, 'You know, this is the first time we've ever clapped eyes on you, really. Your voice and your singing we heard from the boat as it went up and down the river, and we saw you standing on top of that sandbank on Breydon Water, still letting off steam; another time we heard you pass the cabin in good voice.'

'Oh, Mr C, don't remind me, please, that I was nothing but a drunkard in those days.'

At this point Rosie said, 'Don't be so modest, you haven't said the half of it. You weren't just a drunkard, you were a big-head and a womaniser and the most spoilt individual in this world. You must have been born with the idea that you were number one and that you came first in everything, and your command was law. Huh! Calling yourself just a drunkard, that's just the beginning.'

'Oh, Rosie.' Sally shook her head at her, and Fred was laughing too. And now he addressed Charles. 'Do you really know what you have taken on?'

'Yes, Fred, I do; and I've been trying to do so for the last two years. She doesn't know it, but I've chased her around different countries until my feet are sore.'

She moved from him, saying, 'You what?'

'Yes, Mrs Charles McHannen. I've actually known every step you've taken for the last seven years, from the first time we met again. You remember? And you used your old language on me regarding my meanness: I had allowed my ex-wife five million dollars only. You recall?'

Rosie was wide-eyed now as she looked at this man, whom she imagined she had dodged for only two years, until she came to herself during the third year and knew what she really wanted. She cried, in no small voice, 'And you had me followed?'

'No. No, not followed, just taped. I knew what country you would be in and when you were likely to leave, and where you would be making for next; how long you'd be staying there.'

'How did you get to know all that?'

'Believe it or not, my dear Rosie, I am not unknown in the circus in which you moved. Might be news to you but I'm of assistance to them from time to time, and when I need anything they help me.'

Both Fred and Sally sat looking at her. She was really open-mouthed and for the first time, to their knowledge, she was amazed. And then she said slowly, 'Well, as Granda Stevenson would have said – and he never knew what it meant, and neither did I, we only knew it expressed deep feelings at the moment when it was needed – but now I say it, bugger your eyes to hell's flames, Charlie McHannen; and let me add to that, in Mrs Charles McHannen's voice, if I had been acquainted with the fact that you'd had me taped for the last seven years that would have been the last of you.'

'I only followed you for two of them,' put in her husband, 'the last two.'

Impatiently, she shook her head, then said, 'Whatever . . . if I'd known you would not have got me where you did last Saturday morning.'

The ensuing silence was broken by Fred. 'Where was that, Rosie?'

And Rosie replied in the same tone, 'At a blessing before the altar in the church of the Reverend James Watson who himself gave me over to this great big sneaking lout here.' Then she looked directly at Sally and said, 'Having me

taped! Following every step I took. Made legit-
imate. It's going to be some time, I can tell you,
Mrs C, before I get over this. What must they
have thought I was? A Russian spy?'

She rounded on her husband, 'They could
have stopped you. They could, you know,
following me like that, me being in the
Diplomatic Service.'

'You weren't followed, my dearest one. I was
just given the information of where you would
be at certain times, and sometimes I just
happened to be there. The only time that wasn't
arranged was the day I sat down in the tube
beside a strange woman and we recognised each
other. Remember that day?'

Rosie lay back on the couch and closed her
eyes. She was trying hard not to laugh, for now
both the Carpenters and Charles were making
quite a noise in their amusement. Then, nodding
at Fred, Charles said, 'That's the thanks I get. I
bought her that Daimler for a wedding present,
together with the most beautiful gown in Paris,
ready for a ball we're going to next week.'

'I didn't want a damn Daimler. You can keep
it. I'd rather have my old tin can. As for the
gown, I've enough money to buy my own
clothes.'

'Oh, isn't that music to my ears?' Charles was now holding his hands palms out towards the ceiling. 'No woman has ever before said that to me – she has enough money to buy her own clothes. Oh! My dear,' he now swiftly caught hold of her hand and said, 'that is really wonderful news that you can buy your own clothes.'

She pushed him roughly away from her; then looking at Sally and her voice changing, she said, 'That's what we really came down about, the ball; and of course I wanted to show him off,' indicating him with a nod. 'But can you come next weekend and stay with us? It wouldn't be the same if you didn't. It really is going to be our wedding celebration. It's going to be a great get-together, a mixture of all kinds. People I was at school with, people we've both worked with, my family . . . well, from there to umpteen good people from James's parish and the Connolly family, and a number from the factory. Then there are my American in-laws. His father is coming over, and one or two more. I think the one or two more range up to about fifty – I've lost count. I've left all the arrangements to his man. Can you believe that, dear? That he still has to have a man to look after him?'

'Even when he has you?' put in Fred.

'Mr C! I can tell you I'm not looking after anybody else any more in my life; I want to be looked after. I told you that, Mrs C, didn't I? A long time ago. I was tired of looking after people. And, apart from you two, nobody spoke my language or looked after me until now. By the way, the only two I haven't invited are the Fawcetts – let us sock it to you, remember? – who dropped you like a hot brick when at the murder trial they realised you were in sympathy with our family. But I'll have another think about it.'

Then with the most tender look Sally had ever seen on her face Rosie turned and looked at her tall, handsome husband, a man touching his mid-forties, Sally thought. Taking his face between her hands, she said, 'This dear man has promised to give me something that I've known I've wanted for a long time now, and that's a family.'

Fred and Sally had no words to describe the look on Charles McHannen's face. It was alight with love. You could say adoration, and something else that Sally didn't fathom till later, which was humility . . .

* * *

Rosie and Sally were both upstairs saying good night to each other. They had left Fred and Charles smoking cigars downstairs.

They were sitting on the edge of the Carpenters' bed and Rosie asked quietly, 'Were you surprised?'

'Surprised, my dear? Flabbergasted! I still haven't got over it. You know who we expected?'

'No?'

'When a man got on the phone and said he was very, very happy and Rosie would tell us why, of course we never thought about Charlie. Well, who would when the man who was speaking was James Watson?'

Rosie let out a giggle. 'You really thought I was going to marry James?'

'Yes; yes, we did. We love him. He's a good man and we kept telling ourselves when we got over the shock that he was a very good man. Yes; but we had to admit we couldn't really imagine you spending the rest of your life in the East End of London. Oh, really, at times, we couldn't bear the thought; but James seemed so happy.'

'Yes, dear James,' said Rosie. 'He was. He was happy for us both. He was especially happy,

I'm sure, for Charles, for he said to me it was strange the way God worked. He and Peter had played that trick on Charles with the help of his father in the hope that it would let him see there were other ways of living besides his own selfish one. But they never imagined it would have such an effect on him. And you know, Charles had believed this had all happened as it did until just before old Mr Watson died, when something he let slip when Charles was visiting him helped him put two and two together. But he wasn't annoyed at going through what had been really an awful week with the Connollys because they had taught him that people could be happy without money. They also taught him that more than half of the world didn't know how the other half existed, and something inside him urged him to alter his accustomed ways. He has never touched whisky since that night.

'You know, I was attracted to something in him from the first. That night he spoke of our having met years before; I fell for him then, I think. And later, even when I knew he had been married twice, it didn't wipe out the feeling. I thought about those women. They married him for his money, but I have not married him, my dear Mrs C, for his money. I have married him because I love him. I found that out six months ago.'

Rosie leaned towards Sally and put her head on her shoulder, and Sally put her arms around her and listened as she said quietly, 'Oh, I do love him. You said that one day I'd meet someone whom I would love, and I have; and you know, you might think it's silly but I find him wonderful to be with. I only hope it will last.'

'It will last, dear, never fear. Like Fred and me. What we have you two will have, and it will grow with the years.'

THE END

THE BLIND YEARS
by Catherine Cookson

Bridget Gether's parents were killed in the wartime Blitz so she had lived with the Overmeers at Balderstone, their sprawling property in the Northumbrian countryside, since she was a child. Unaware that she had been manipulated into agreeing to marry their son Laurence, an encounter with Bruce Dickenson, the son of a neighbouring farmer, opened her eyes to the possibility that she might be making a serious mistake.

Although Bridget told herself she had loved Laurence for years, could she now trust him? *Had* he been seeing someone else all the time he had been courting her? She decided that there were sufficient grounds for doubt, so she called off the marriage.

However, she had reckoned without the formidable Overmeer family, whose desperate financial straits compelled them to take steps to protect their interests. As for Laurence, he could not forgive Bridget for the humiliation of rejection, so he made his own plans to punish her. But someone else was also planning revenge, the outcome of which would shake the very foundations of the Overmeer family.

0 552 14609 9

RILEY
by Catherine Cookson

There were many who said that Riley appeared to be older than his years. He finished school at an early age, leaving a harsh childhood behind him, brimful of optimism and secure in the knowledge that his teacher, Fred Beardsley, had faith in him. Neither of them could have envisaged at the time how their lives would be intertwined.

Fred encouraged Riley, a gifted mimic, when he was offered a position at The Little Palace Theatre in Fellburn. And then Riley surprised Fred by forming a close friendship with leading lady, Nyrene Forbes-Mason, who was nurturing his burgeoning talent as an actor. What Riley hadn't told him was that he had great hopes of the relationship developing into something more.

Over the subsequent years, Fred observed with amazement Riley's rise to fame and fortune. As for his relationship with Nyrene, that did indeed change although not in the way that Riley had envisaged.

0 552 14155 0